ANTHONY POWELL

The Acceptance World

A Novel

FONTANA BOOKS
BY AGREEMENT WITH
HEINEMANN

First published in 1955 by William Heinemann Ltd
First issued in Fontana Books 1967
Second Impression October 1968
Third Impression December 1972
Fourth Impression December 1974
Sixth Impression September 1977

© Anthony Powell 1955

Made and printed in Great Britain by
William Collins Sons & Co Ltd Glasgow

CONDITIONS OF SALE
This book is sold subject to the condition
that it shall not, by way of trade or otherwise,
be lent, re-sold, hired out or otherwise circulated
without the publisher's prior consent in any form of
binding or cover other than that in which it is
published and without a similar condition
including this condition being imposed
on the subsequent purchaser

For Adrian

ONE

Once in a way, perhaps as often as every eighteen months, an invitation to Sunday afternoon tea at the Ufford would arrive on a postcard addressed in Uncle Giles's neat, constricted handwriting. This private hotel in Bayswater, where he stayed during comparatively rare visits to London, occupied two corner houses in a latent, almost impenetrable region west of the Queen's Road. Not only the battleship-grey colour, but also something at once angular and top-heavy about the block's configuration as a whole, suggested a large vessel moored in the street. Even within, at least on the ground floor, the Ufford conveyed some reminder of life at sea, though certainly of no luxuriously equipped liner; at best one of those superannuated schooners of Conrad's novels, perhaps decorated years before as a rich man's yacht, now tarnished by the years and reduced to ignoble uses like traffic in tourists, pilgrims, or even illegal immigrants; pervaded—to borrow an appropriately Conradian mannerism—with uneasy memories of the strife of men. That was the feeling the Ufford gave, riding at anchor on the sluggish Bayswater tides.

To this last retrospective, and decidedly depressing, aspect of the hotel's character, Uncle Giles himself had no doubt in a small degree contributed. Certainly he had done nothing to release the place from its air of secret, melancholy guilt. The passages seemed catacombs of a hell assigned to the subdued regret of those who had lacked in life the income to which they felt themselves entitled; this sus-

picion that the two houses were an abode of the dead being increased by the fact that no one was ever to be seen about, even at the reception desk. The floors of the formerly separate buildings, constructed at different levels, were now joined by unexpected steps and narrow, steeply slanting passages. The hall was always wrapped in silence; letters in the green baize board criss-crossed with tape remained yellowing, for ever unclaimed, unread, unchanged.

However, Uncle Giles himself was attached to these quarters. "The old pub suits me," I had once heard him mutter thickly under his breath, high commendation from one so sparing of praise; although of course the Ufford, like every other institution with which he came in contact, would fall into disfavour from time to time, usually on account of some "incivility" offered him by the management or staff. For example, Vera, a waitress, was an old enemy, who would often attempt to exclude him from his favourite table by the door "where you could get a breath of air." At least once, in a fit of pique, he had gone to the De Tabley across the road; but sooner or later he was back again, grudgingly admitting that the Ufford, although going downhill from the days when he had first known the establishment, was undoubtedly convenient for the purposes of his aimless, uncomfortable, but in a sense dedicated life.

Dedicated, it might well be asked, to what? The question would not be easy to answer. Dedicated, perhaps, to his own egotism; his determination to be—without adequate moral or intellectual equipment—absolutely different from everybody else. That might offer one explanation of his behaviour. At any rate, he was propelled along from pillar to post by some force that seemed stronger than a mere instinct to keep himself alive; and the Ufford was the nearest thing he recognised as a home. He would leave

his luggage there for weeks, months, even years on end; complaining afterwards, when he unpacked, that dinner-jackets were not only creased but also ravaged by moth, or that oil had been allowed to soak through the top of his cane trunk and ruin the tropical clothing within; still worse—though exact proof was always lacking—that the pieces left in the hotel's keeping had actually been reduced in number by at least one canvas valise, leather hat-box, or uniform-case in black tin.

On most of the occasions when I visited the Ufford, halls and reception rooms were so utterly deserted that the interior might almost have been Uncle Giles's private residence. Had he been a rich bachelor, instead of a poor one, he would probably have lived in a house of just that sort: bare: anonymous: old-fashioned: draughty: with heavy mahogany cabinets and sideboards spaced out at intervals in passages and on landings; nothing that could possibly commit him to any specific opinion, beyond general disapproval of the way the world was run.

We always had tea in an apartment called " the lounge," the back half of a large double drawing-room, the inner doors of which were kept permanently closed, thus detaching " the lounge " from " the writing-room," the half over-looking the street. (Perhaps, like the doors of the Temple of Janus, they were closed only in time of Peace; because, years later, when I saw the Ufford in war-time these particular doors had been thrown wide open.) The lace-curtained windows of the lounge gave on to a well; a bleak outlook, casting the gloom of perpetual night, or of a sky for ever dark with rain. Even in summer the electric light had to be switched on during tea.

The wallpaper's intricate floral design in blue, grey and green ran upwards from a cream-coloured Lincrusta dado to a cornice also of cream Lincrusta. The pattern of flowers,

infinitely faded, closely matched the chintz-covered sofa
and arm-chairs, which were roomy and unexpectedly comfortable. A palm in a brass pot with ornamental handles
stood in one corner: here and there were small tables of
Moorish design upon each of which had been placed a
heavy white globular ash-tray, equipped with an attachment
upon which to rest a cigar or cigarette. Several circular
gilt looking-glasses hung about the walls, but there was
only one picture, an engraving placed over the fireplace, of
Landseer's *Bolton Abbey in the Olden Time*. Beneath this
crowded scene of medieval plenty—presenting a painful
contrast with the Ufford's *cuisine*—a clock, so constructed
that pendulum and internal works were visible under its
glass dome, stood eternally at twenty minutes past five.
Two radiators kept the room reasonably warm in winter,
and the coal, surrounded in the fireplace with crinkled pink
paper, was never alight. No sign of active life was apparent in the room except for several much-thumbed copies of
The Lady lying in a heap on one of the Moorish tables.

" I think we shall have this place to ourselves," Uncle
Giles used invariably to remark, as if we had come there by
chance on a specially lucky day, " so that we shall be able
to talk over our business without disturbance. Nothing I
hate more than having some damn'd fellow listening to
every word I say."

Of late years his affairs, in so far as his relatives knew
anything of them, had become to some extent stabilised,
although invitations to tea were inclined to coincide with
periodical efforts to extract slightly more than his agreed
share from " the Trust." Either his path had grown more
tranquil than formerly, or crises were at longer intervals
and apparently less violent. This change did not imply
that he approached life itself in a more conciliatory spirit,

or had altered his conviction that worldly success was a matter of "influence." The country's abandonment of the Gold Standard at about this time—and the formation of the National Government—had particularly annoyed him. He propagated contrary, and far more revolutionary, economic theories of his own as to how the European monetary situation should be regulated.

He was, however, a shade less abrupt in personal dealings. The anxiety of his relations that he might one day get into a really serious financial tangle, never entirely at rest, had considerably abated in comparison with time past; nor had there been recently any of those once recurrent rumours that he was making preparations for an unsuitable marriage. He still hovered about the Home Counties, seen intermittently at Reading, Aylesbury, Chelmsford, or Dover—and once so far afield as the Channel Islands—his "work" now connected with the administration of some charitable organisation which paid a small salary and allowed a reasonably high expense account.

I was not sure, however, in the light of an encounter during one of my visits to the Ufford, that Uncle Giles, although by then just about in his sixties, had wholly relinquished all thought of marriage. There were circumstances that suggested a continued interest in such a project, or at least that he still enjoyed playing with the idea of matrimony when in the company of the opposite sex.

On that particular occasion, the three fish-paste sandwiches and slice of seed cake finished, talk about money was about to begin. Uncle Giles himself never ate tea, though he would usually remove the lid of the teapot on its arrival and comment: "A good sergeant-major's brew you've got there," sometimes sending the tea back to the kitchen if something about the surface of the liquid speci-

ally displeased him. He had blown his nose once or twice as a preliminary to financial discussion, when the door of the lounge quietly opened and a lady wearing a large hat and purple dress came silently into the room.

She was between forty and fifty, perhaps nearer fifty, though possibly her full bosom and style of dress, at a period when it was fashionable to be thin, made her seem a year or two older than her age. Dark red hair piled high on her head in what seemed to me an outmoded style, and good, curiously blurred features from which looked out immense, misty, hazel eyes, made her appearance striking. Her movements, too, were unusual. She seemed to glide rather than walk across the carpet, giving the impression almost of a phantom, a being from another world; this illusion no doubt heightened by the mysterious, sombre *ambience* of the Ufford, and the fact that I had scarcely ever before seen anybody but Uncle Giles himself, or an occasional member of the hotel's staff, inhabit its rooms.

"Why, Myra," said Uncle Giles, rising hurriedly, and smoothing the worn herring-bone tweed of his trouser leg, "I thought you said you were going to be out all day."

He sounded on the whole pleased to see her, although perhaps a trifle put out that she should have turned up just at that moment. He would very occasionally, and with due warning, produce an odd male acquaintance for a minute or two, never longer, usually an elderly man, probably a retired accountant, said to possess "a very good head for business," but never before had I seen him in the company of a woman not a member of the family. Now as usual his habitual air of hardly suppressed irritation tended to cloak any minor emotion by the strength of its cosmic resentment. All the same, a very rare thing with him, faint patches of colour showed for a moment in his cheeks, disappearing almost immediately, as he fingered his mous-

tache with a withered, skinny hand, as if uncertain how best to approach the situation.

"This is my nephew Nicholas," he said; and to me: "I don't think you have met Mrs. Erdleigh."

He spoke slowly, as if, after much thought, he had chosen me from an immense number of other nephews to show her at least one good example of what he was forced to endure in the way of relatives. Mrs. Erdleigh gazed at me for a second or two before taking my hand, continuing to encircle its fingers even after I had made a slight effort to relax my own grasp. Her palm felt warm and soft, and seemed to exude a mysterious tremor. Scent, vaguely Oriental in its implications, rolled across from her in great stifling waves. The huge liquid eyes seemed to look deep down into my soul, and far, far beyond towards nameless, unexplored vistas of the infinite.

"But he belongs to another order," she stated at once.

She spoke without surprise and apparently quite decisively; indeed as if the conclusion had been the logical inference of our hands' prolonged contact. At the same time she turned her head towards Uncle Giles, who made a deprecatory sound in his throat, though without venturing to confirm or deny her hypothesis. It was evident that he and I were placed violently in contrast together in her mind, or rather, I supposed, her inner consciousness. Whether she referred to some indefinable difference of class or bearing, or whether the distinction was in moral standards, was not at all clear. Nor had I any idea whether the comparison was in my uncle's favour or my own. In any case I could not help feeling that the assertion, however true, was untimely as an opening gambit after introduction.

I had half expected Uncle Giles to take offence at the words, but, on the contrary, he seemed not at all annoyed or surprised; even appearing rather more resigned than

before to Mrs. Erdleigh's presence. It was almost as if he now knew that the worst was over; that from this moment relations between the three of us would grow easier.

"Shall I ring for some more tea?" he asked, without in any way pressing the proposal by tone of voice.

Mrs. Erdleigh shook her head dreamily. She had taken the place beside me on the sofa.

"I have already had tea," she said softly, as if that meal had been for her indeed a wonderful experience.

"Are you sure?" asked my uncle, wonderingly; confirming by his manner that such a phenomenon was scarcely credible.

"Truly."

"Well, I won't, then."

"No, please, Captain Jenkins."

I had the impression that the two of them knew each other pretty well; certainly much better than either was prepared at that moment to admit in front of me. After the first surprise of seeing her, Uncle Giles no longer called Mrs. Erdleigh "Myra," and he now began to utter a disconnected series of conventional remarks, as if to display how formal was in fact their relationship. He explained for the hundredth time how he never took tea as a meal, however much encouraged by those addicted to the habit, commented in desultory phrases on the weather, and sketched in for her information a few of the outward circumstances of my own life and employment.

"Art books, is it?" he said. "Is that what you told me your firm published?"

"That's it."

"He sells art books," said Uncle Giles, as if he were explaining to some visitor the strange habits of the aborigines in the land where he had chosen to settle.

" And other sorts too," I added, since he made the publication of art books sound so shameful a calling.

In answering, I addressed myself to Mrs. Erdleigh, rather in the way that a witness, cross-questioned by counsel, replies to the judge. She seemed hardly to take in these trivialities, though she smiled all the while, quietly, almost rapturously, rather as if she were enjoying a warm bath after a trying day's shopping. I noticed that she wore no wedding ring, carrying in its place on her third finger a large opal, enclosed by a massive gold serpent swallowing its own tail.

" I see you are wondering about my opal," she said, suddenly catching my eye.

" I was admiring the ring."

" Of course I was born in October."

" Otherwise it would be unlucky?"

" But *not* under the Scales."

" I am the Archer."

I had learned that fact a week or two before from the astrological column of a Sunday newspaper. This seemed a good moment to make use of the knowledge. Mrs. Erdleigh was evidently pleased even with this grain of esoteric apprehension. She took my hand once more, and held the open palm towards the light.

" You interest me," she said.

" What do you see?"

" Many things."

" Nice ones?"

" Some good, some less good."

" Tell me about them."

" Shall I?"

Uncle Giles fidgeted. I thought at first he was bored at being momentarily out of the conversation, because, in his

self-contained, unostentatious way, he could never bear to be anything less than the centre of interest; even when that position might possess an unpleasant significance as sometimes happened at family gatherings. However, another matter was on his mind.

" Why not put the cards out? " he broke in all at once with forced cheerfulness. " That is, if you're in the mood."

Mrs. Erdleigh did not reply immediately to this suggestion. She continued to smile, and to investigate the lines of my palm.

" Shall I? " she again said softly, almost to herself. " Shall I ask the cards about you both? "

I added my request to my uncle's. To have one's fortune told gratifies, after all, most of the superficial demands of egotism. There is no mystery about the eternal popularity of divination. All the same, I was surprised that Uncle Giles should countenance such pursuits. I felt sure he would have expressed loud contempt if anyone else had been described to him as indulging in efforts to foretell the future. Mrs. Erdleigh pondered a few seconds, then rose, still smiling, and glided away across the room. When she had shut the door we remained in silence for some minutes. Uncle Giles grunted several times. I suspected he might be feeling rather ashamed of himself for having put this request to her. I made some enquiries about his friend.

" Myra Erdleigh? " he said, as if it were strange to meet anyone unaware of Mrs. Erdleigh's circumstances. " She's a widow, of course. Husband did something out in the East. Chinese Customs, was it? Burma Police? Something of the sort."

" And she lives here? "

" A wonderful fortune-teller," said Uncle Giles, ignoring the last question. " Really wonderful. I let her tell mine once in a while. It gives her pleasure, you know—and it

interests me to see how often she is right. Not that I expect she will have much to promise me at my time of life."

He sighed; though not, I thought, without a certain self-satisfaction. I wondered how long they had known one another. Long enough, apparently, for the question of fortune-telling to have cropped up between them a number of times.

" Does she tell fortunes professionally?"

" Has done, I believe, in the past," Uncle Giles admitted. " But of course there wouldn't be any question of a five guinea consultation fee this evening."

He gave a short angry laugh, to show that he was joking, adding rather guiltily: " I don't think anyone is likely to come in. Even if they did, we could always pretend we were taking a hand at cut-throat."

I wondered if Mrs. Erdleigh used Tarot cards. If so, three-handed bridge might not look very convincing to an intruder; for example, should one of us try to trump " the drowned Phœnician Sailor " with " the Hanged Man." In any case, there seemed no reason why we should not have our fortunes told in the lounge. That would at least be employing the room to some purpose. The manner in which Uncle Giles had spoken made me think he must enjoy " putting the cards out " more than he cared to acknowledge.

Mrs. Erdleigh did not come back to the room immediately. We awaited her return in an atmosphere of expectancy induced by my uncle's unconcealed excitement. I had never before seen him in this state. He was breathing heavily. Still Mrs. Erdleigh did not appear. She must have remained away at least ten minutes or a quarter of an hour. Uncle Giles began humming to himself. I picked up one of the tattered copies of *The Lady*. At last the door opened

once more. Mrs. Erdleigh had removed her hat, renewed
the blue make-up under her eyes, and changed into a dress
of sage green. She was certainly a conspicuous, perhaps
even a faintly sinister figure. The cards she brought with
her were grey and greasy with use. They were not a Tarot
pack. After a brief discussion it was agreed that Uncle
Giles should be the first to look into the future.

"You don't think it has been too short an interval?" he
asked, obviously with some last-moment apprehensions.

"Nearly six months," said Mrs. Erdleigh, in a more
matter-of-fact voice than that she had used hitherto; adding, as she began to shuffle the pack: "Although, of
course, one should not question the cards too often, as I
have sometimes warned you."

Uncle Giles slowly rubbed his hands together, watching
her closely as if to make certain there was no deception, and
to ensure that she did not deliberately slip in a card that
would bring him bad luck. The rite had something solemn
about it: something infinitely ancient, as if Mrs. Erdleigh
had existed long before the gods we knew, even those belonging to the most distant past. I asked if she always used
the same pack.

"Always the same dear cards," she said, smiling; and to
my uncle, more seriously: "Was there anything special?"

"Usually need to look ahead in business," he said, gruffly.
"That would be Diamonds, I suppose. Or Clubs?"

Mrs. Erdleigh continued to smile without revealing any
of her secrets, while she set the cards in various small heaps
on one of the Moorish tables. Uncle Giles kept a sharp
eye on her, still rubbing his hands, making me almost as
nervous as himself at the thought of what the predictions
could involve. There might always be grave possibilities
to be faced for someone of his erratic excursion through
life. However, I was naturally much more interested in

what she would say about myself. Indeed, I was then so far from grasping the unchanging mould of human nature that I found it even surprising that at his age he could presuppose anything to be called "a future." So far as I myself was concerned, on the other hand, there seemed no reason to curb the wildest absurdity of fancy as to what might happen the very next moment.

However, when Uncle Giles's cards were examined, their secrets did not appear to be anything like so ominous as might have been feared. There was a good deal of opposition to his "plans," perhaps not surprisingly; also, it was true, much gossip, even some calumny surrounded him.

"Don't forget you have Saturn in the Twelfth House," Mrs. Erdleigh remarked in an aside. "Secret enemies."

As against these threatening possibilities, someone was going to give him a present, probably money; a small sum, but acceptable. It looked as if this gift might come from a woman. Uncle Giles, whose cheeks had become furrowed at the thought of all the gossip and calumny, cheered up a little at this. He was told he had a good friend in a woman —possibly the one who was to make him a present—the Queen of Hearts, in fact. This, too, Uncle Giles accepted willingly enough.

"That was the marriage card that turned up, wasn't it?" he asked at one point.

"Could be."

"Not necessarily?"

"Other influences must be taken into consideration."

Neither of them commented on this matter, though their words evidently had regard to a question already reconnoitred in the past. For a moment or two there was perhaps a faint sense of additional tension. Then the cards were collected and shuffled again.

" Now let's hear about *him*," said Uncle Giles.

He spoke more with relief that his own ordeal was over, rather than because he was seriously expressing any burning interest in my own fate.

" I expect *he* wants to hear about *love*," said Mrs. Erdleigh, beginning to titter to herself again.

Uncle Giles, to show general agreement with this supposition, grunted a disapproving laugh. I attempted some formal denial, although it was perfectly true that the thought was uppermost in my mind. The situation in that quarter was at the moment confused. In fact, so far as " love " was concerned, I had been living for some years past in a rather makeshift manner. This was not because I felt the matter to be of little interest, like a man who hardly cares what he eats provided hunger is satisfied, or one prepared to discuss painting, should the subject arise, though never tempted to enter a picture gallery. On the contrary, my interest in love was keen enough, but the thing itself seemed not particularly simple to come by. In that direction, other people appeared more easily satisfied than myself. That at least was how it seemed to me. And yet, in spite of some show of picking and choosing, my experiences, on subsequent examination, were certainly no more admirable than those to which neither Templer nor Barnby, for example, would have given a second thought; they were merely fewer in number. I hoped the cards would reveal nothing too humiliating to my own self-esteem.

" There is a link between us," said Mrs. Erdleigh, as she set out the little heaps. " At present I cannot see what it is —but there is a link."

This supposed connection evidently puzzled her.

" You are musical?"

" No."

" Then you write—I think you have written a book?"

" Yes."

" You live between two worlds," she said. " Perhaps even more than two worlds. You cannot always surmount your feelings."

I could think of no possible reply to this indictment.

" You are thought cold, but you possess deep affections, sometimes for people worthless in themselves. Often you are at odds with those who might help you. You like women, and they like you, but you often find the company of men more amusing. You expect too much, and yet you are also too resigned. You must try to understand life."

Somewhat awed by this searching, even severe analysis, I promised I would do better in future.

" People can only be themselves," she said. " If they possessed the qualities you desire in them, they would be different people."

" That is what I should like them to be."

" Sometimes you are too serious, sometimes not serious enough."

" So I have been told."

" You must make a greater effort in life."

" I can see that."

These strictures certainly seemed just enough; and yet any change of direction would be hard to achieve. Perhaps I was irrevocably transfixed, just as she described, halfway between dissipation and diffidence. While I considered the matter, she passed on to more circumstantial things. It turned out that a fair woman was not very pleased with me; and a dark one almost equally vexed. Like my uncle—perhaps some family failing common to both of us—I was encompassed by gossip.

" They do not signify at all," said Mrs. Erdleigh, refer-

ring thus rather ruthlessly to the women of disparate colour-ing. " This is a much more important lady—medium hair, I should say—and I think you have run across her once or twice before, though not recently. But there seems to be another man interested, too. He might even be a husband. You don't like him much. He is tallish, I should guess. Fair, possibly red hair. In business. Often goes abroad."

I began to turn over in my mind every woman I had ever met.

" There is a small matter in *your* business that is going to cause inconvenience," she went on. " It has to do with an elderly man—and two young ones connected with him."

" Are you sure it is not two elderly men and one young man?"

It had immediately struck me that she might be *en rapport* with my firm's growing difficulties regarding St. John Clarke's introduction to *The Art of Horace Isbister*. The elderly men would be St. John Clarke and Isbister themselves—or perhaps St. John Clarke and one of the partners—and the young man was, of course, St. John Clarke's secretary, Mark Members.

" I see the two young men quite plainly," she said. " Rather a troublesome couple, I should say."

This was all credible enough, including the character sketch, though perhaps not very interesting. Such trivial comment, mixed with a few home truths of a personal nature, provide, I had already learnt, the commonplaces of fortune-telling. Such was all that remained in my mind of what Mrs. Erdleigh prophesied on that occasion. She may have foretold more. If so, her words were forgotten by me. Indeed, I was not greatly struck by the insight she had shown; although she impressed me as a woman of domi-nant, even oddly attractive personality, in spite of a certain

absurdity of demeanour. She herself seemed well pleased with the performance.

At the end of her sitting it was time to go. I was dining that evening with Barnby, picking him up at his studio. I rose to say good-bye, thanking her for the trouble she had taken.

" We shall meet again."

" I hope so."

" In about a year from now."

" Perhaps before."

" No," she said, smiling with the complacence of one to whom the secrets of human existence had been long since occultly revealed. " Not before."

I did not press the point. Uncle Giles accompanied me to the hall. He had by then returned to the subject of money, the *mystique* of which was at least as absorbing to him as the rites upon which we had been engaged.

" . . . and then one could not foresee that San Pedro Warehouses Deferred would become entirely valueless," he was saying. " The expropriations were merely the result of a liberal dictator coming in—got to face these changes. There was one of those quite natural revulsions against foreign capital. . . ."

He broke off. Supposing our meeting now at an end, I turned from him, and made preparations to plunge through the opaque doors into the ocean of streets, in the grey ebb and flow of which the Ufford floated idly upon the swell. Uncle Giles put his hand on my arm.

" By the way," he said, " I don't think I should mention to your parents the matter of having your fortune told. I don't want them to blame me for leading you into bad habits, superstitious ones, I mean. Besides, they might not altogether approve of Myra Erdleigh."

His brown, wrinkled face puckered slightly. He still retained some vestige of good looks, faintly military in character. Perhaps this hint, increased with age, of past regimental distinction in some forgotten garrison town was what Mrs. Erdleigh admired in him. Neither my parents, nor any of the rest of Uncle Giles's relations, were likely to worry about his behaviour if the worst he ever did was to persuade other members of the family to have their fortunes told. However, recognising that silence upon the subject of Mrs. Erdleigh might be a reasonable request, I assured him that I would not speak of our meeting.

I was curious to know what their relationship might be. Possibly they were planning marriage. The " marriage card " had clearly been of interest to my uncle. There was something vaguely " improper " about Mrs. Erdleigh, almost deliberately so; but impropriety of an unremembered, Victorian kind: a villa in St. John's Wood, perhaps, and eccentric doings behind locked doors and lace curtains on sultry summer afternoons. Uncle Giles was known to possess a capacity for making himself acceptable to ladies of all sorts, some of whom had even been rumoured to contribute at times a trifle towards his expenses; those many expenses to which he was subject, and never tired of detailing. Mrs. Erdleigh looked not so much " well off " as eminently capable of pursuing her own interests effectively. Possibly Uncle Giles considered her a good investment. She, on her side, no doubt had her uses for him. Apart from material considerations, he was obviously fascinated by her occult powers, with which he seemed almost religiously preoccupied. Like all such associations, this one probably included a fierce struggle of wills. It would be interesting to see who won the day. On the whole, my money was on Mrs. Erdleigh. I thought about the pair of

them for a day or two, and then they both passed from my mind.

As I made my way towards the neighbourhood of Fitzroy Square, experiencing as usual that feeling of release that always followed parting company with Uncle Giles, I returned to the subject of future business difficulties foretold in the cards. These, as I have said, had seemed to refer to St. John Clarke's introduction to *The Art of Horace Isbister*, already a tiresome affair, quite likely to pass from bad to worse. The introduction had been awaited for at least a year now, and we seemed no nearer getting the manuscript. The delay caused inconvenience at the office, since blocks had been made for a series of forty-eight monochrome plates and four three-colour half-tones; to which St. John Clarke was to add four or five thousand words of biographical reminiscence.

Isbister himself had been ill, on and off, for some little time, so that it had not been possible through him to bring pressure to bear on St. John Clarke, although the painter was the novelist's old friend. They may even have been at school together. Isbister had certainly executed several portraits of St. John Clarke, one of them (the sitter in a high, stiff collar and limp spotted bow tie) showing him as quite a young man. The personal legend of each, for publicity purposes, took the form of a country lad who had " made good," and they would occasionally refer in print to their shared early struggles. St. John Clarke, in the first instance, had positively gone out of his way to arrange that the introduction should be written by himself, rather than by some suitable hack from amongst the Old Guard of the art critics, several of whom were in much more need of the fee, not a very princely one, that my firm was paying for the work.

That a well-known novelist should take on something that seemed to call in at least a small degree for an accredited expert on painting was not so surprising as might at first sight have appeared, because St. John Clarke, although certainly quieter of late years, had in the past often figured in public controversy regarding the arts. He had been active, for example, in the years before the war in supporting the erection of the Peter Pan statue in Kensington Gardens: a dozen years later, vigorously opposing the establishment of Rima in the bird sanctuary of the same neighbourhood. At one of the Walpole-Wilsons' dinner parties I could remember talk of St. John Clarke's intervention in the question of the Haig memorial, then much discussed. These examples suggest a special interest in sculpture, but St. John Clarke often expressed himself with equal force regarding painting and music. He had certainly been associated with opposition to the Post-Impressionists in 1910: also in leading some minor skirmish in operatic circles soon after the Armistice.

I myself could not have denied a taste for St. John Clarke's novels at about the period when leaving school. In fact Le Bas, my housemaster, finding me reading one of them, had taken it from my hand and glanced through the pages.

" Rather morbid stuff, isn't it?" he had remarked.

It was a statement rather than a question, though I doubt whether Le Bas had ever read any of St. John Clarke's novels himself. He merely felt, in one sense correctly, that there was something wrong with them. At the same time he made no attempt to disallow, or confiscate, the volume. However, I had long preferred to forget the days when I had regarded St. John Clarke's work as fairly daring. In fact I had become accustomed to refer to him and his books with the savagery which, when one is a young man, seems

—perhaps rightly—the only proper and serious attitude towards anyone, most of all an older person, practising the arts in an inept or outworn manner.

Although a few years younger than the generation of H. G. Wells and J. M. Barrie, St. John Clarke was connected in my mind with those two authors, chiefly because I had once seen a snapshot of the three of them reproduced in the memoirs of an Edwardian hostess. The photograph had probably been taken by the lady herself. The writers were standing in a group on the lawn of a huge, rather gracelessly pinnacled country seat. St. John Clarke was a little to one side of the picture. A tall, cadaverous man, with spectacles and long hair, a panama hat at the back of his head, he leant on a stick, surveying his more diminutive fellow guests with an expression of uneasy interest; rather as if he were an explorer or missionary, who had just coaxed from the jungle these powerful witch-doctors of some neighbouring, and on the whole unfriendly, tribe. He seemed, by his expression, to feel that constant supervision of the other two was necessary to foil misbehaviour or escape. There was something of the priest about his appearance.

The picture had interested me because, although I had already read books by these three writers, all had inspired me with the same sense that theirs was not the kind of writing I liked. Later, as I have said, I came round for a time to St. John Clarke with that avid literary consumption of the immature which cannot precisely be regarded either as enjoyment or the reverse. The flavour of St. John Clarke's novels is hard to describe to those unfamiliar with them, perhaps on account of their own inexactitudes of thought and feeling. Although no longer looked upon as a " serious " writer, I believe he still has his readers in number not to be disregarded. In his early years he had

been treated with respect by most of the eminent critics of his time, and to the day of his death he hoped in vain for the Nobel Prize. Mark Members, his secretary, used to say that once, at least, that award had seemed within his grasp.

We had never met, but I had seen him in Bond Street, walking with Members. Though his hair was by then white and straggling, he still looked remarkably like his picture in the book of memoirs. He was wearing a grey soft hat, rather high in the crown with a band of the same colour, a black suit and buff double-breasted waistcoat. As he strolled along he glanced rather furtively about him, seeming scarcely aware of Members, sauntering by his side. His features bore that somewhat exasperated expression that literary men so often acquire in middle life. For a second I had been reminded of my old acquaintance, Mr. Deacon, but a Mr. Deacon far more capable of coping with the world. Members, in his black homburg, swinging a rolled umbrella, looked quite boyish beside him.

St. John Clarke's reputation as a novelist had been made by the time he was in his thirties. For many years past he had lived the life of a comparatively rich bachelor, able to indulge most of his whims, seeing only the people who suited him, and making his way in what he used to call, "rather lovingly," so Members said, the "*beau monde*." Even in those days, critics malicious enough to pull his books to pieces in public were never tired of pointing out that investigations of human conduct, based on assumptions accepted when St. John Clarke was a young man, were hopelessly out of date. However, fortunately his sales did not depend on favourable reviews, although, in spite of this, he was said to be—like so many financially successful writers—painfully sensitive to hostile criticism. It was perhaps partly for the reason that he felt himself no longer properly appreciated that he had announced he would

write no more novels. In due course memoirs would appear, though he confessed he was in no hurry to compose them.

His procrastination regarding the introduction had, therefore, nothing to do with pressure of work. Putting the Isbister task in its least idealistic and disinterested light, it would give him a chance to talk about himself, a perfectly legitimate treat he was as a rule unwilling to forgo. Friendship made him a suitable man for the job. Those who enjoy finding landmarks common to different forms of art might even have succeeded in tracing a certain similarity of approach tenuously relating the novels of St. John Clarke with the portrait painting of Isbister. The delay was, indeed, hard to explain.

There had been, however, various rumours recently current regarding changes supposedly taking place in St. John Clarke's point of view. Lately, he had been seen at parties in Bloomsbury, and elsewhere, surrounded by people who were certainly not readers of his books. This was thought to show the influence of Members, who was said to be altering his employer's outlook. Indeed, something suggesting a change of front in that quarter had been brought to my own notice in a very personal manner.

St. John Clarke had contributed an article to a New York paper in which he spoke of the younger writers of that moment. Amongst a rather oddly assorted collection of names, he had commented, at least by implication favourably, upon a novel of my own, published a month or two before—the " book " to which Mrs. Erdleigh had referred. Latterly, St. John Clarke had rarely occupied himself with occasional journalism, and in print he had certainly never before shown himself well disposed towards a younger generation. His remarks, brief and relatively guarded though they had been, not unnaturally aroused my interest,

especially because any recommendation from that quarter was so entirely unexpected. I found myself looking for excuses to cover what still seemed to me his own short-comings as a novelist.

As I turned over these things in my mind, on the way to Barnby's studio, it struck me that Barnby himself might be able to tell me something of St. John Clarke as a person; for, although unlikely that Barnby had read the novels, the two of them might well have met in the widely different circles Barnby frequented. I began to make en-quiries soon after my arrival there.

Barnby rubbed his short, stubby hair, worn *en brosse,* which, with his blue overalls, gave him the look of a *sommelier* at an expensive French restaurant. By then we had known each other for several years. He had moved house more than once since the days when he had lived above Mr. Deacon's antique shop, emigrating for a time as far north as Camden Town. Still unmarried, his many adventures with women were a perpetual topic between us. In terms of literature, Barnby might have found a place among Stendhal's heroes, those power-conscious young men, anxious to achieve success with women without the banal expedient of "falling in love:" a state, of course, necessarily implying, on the part of the competitor, a depletion, if not entire abrogation, of "the will." Barnby was, on the whole, more successful than his Stendhalian prototypes, and he was certainly often "in love." All the same, he belonged in that group. Like Valmont in *Les Liaisons Dangereuses*, he set store "upon what terms" he possessed a woman, seeking a relationship in which sensu-ality merged with power, rather than engaging in their habitual conflict.

Like everyone else, at that moment, Barnby was com-plaining of "the slump," although his own reputation as a

painter had been rising steadily during the previous two or three years. The murals designed by him for the Donners-Brebner Building had received, one way and another, a great deal of public attention; the patronage of Sir Magnus Donners himself in this project having even survived Barnby's love affair with Baby Wentworth, supposed mistress of Sir Magnus. Indeed, it had been suggested that " the Great Industrialist," as Barnby used to call him, had been glad to make use of that or some other indiscretion, soon after the completion of the murals, as an excuse for bringing to an end his own association with Mrs. Wentworth. There appeared to be no bad feeling between any of the persons concerned in this triangular adjustment. Sir Magnus was now seen about with a *jolie laide* called Matilda Wilson; although, as formerly in the Baby Wentworth connection, little or nothing definite was known of this much discussed liaison. Baby herself had married an Italian and was living in Rome.

" You'll never get that introduction now," Barnby said, after listening to my story. " St. John Clarke in these days would think poor old Isbister much too *pompier*."

" But they are still great friends."

" What does that matter?"

" Besides, St. John Clarke doesn't know a Van Dyck from a Van Dongen."

" Ah, but he does now," said Barnby. " That's where you are wrong. You are out of date. St. John Clarke has undergone a conversion."

" To what?"

" Modernism."

" Steel chairs?"

" No doubt they will come."

" Pictures made of shells and newspaper?"

" At present he is at a slightly earlier stage."

I asked for further details.

"The outward and visible sign of St. John Clarke's conversion," said Barnby, portentously, "is that he has indeed become a collector of modern pictures—though, as I understand it, he still loves them on this side Surrealism. As a matter of fact he bought a picture of mine last week."

"This conversion explains his friendly notice of my book."

"It does."

"I see."

"You yourself supposed that something unusual in the quality of your writing had touched him?"

"Naturally."

"I fear it is all part of a much larger design."

"Just as good for me."

"Doubtless."

All the same, I felt slightly less complimented than before. The situation was now clear. The rumours already current about St. John Clarke, less explicit than Barnby's words, had equally suggested some kind of intellectual upheaval. Isbister's portraits of politicians, business men and ecclesiastics, executed with emphatic, almost aggressive disregard for any development of painting that could possibly be called "modern", would now certainly no longer appeal to his old friend. At the same time the ray of St. John Clarke's approval directed towards myself, until then so phenomenal, was in fact only one minute aspect of the novelist's new desire to ally himself with forces against which, for many years, he had openly warred.

"That secretary of his even suggested Clarke might commission a portrait."

"It is Members, of course, who has brought this about."

"Oh, I don't know," said Barnby. "This sort of thing often happens to successful people when they begin to get

old. They suddenly realise what dull lives they have always led."

"But St. John Clarke hasn't led a dull life. I should have thought he had done almost everything he wanted—with just sufficient heights still to climb to give continued zest to his efforts."

"I agree in one sense," said Barnby. "But for a man of his comparative intelligence, St. John Clarke has always limited himself to the dullest of dull ideas—in order to make money, of course, a very reasonable aim, thereby avoiding giving offence to his public. Think of the platitudes of his books. True, I have only read a few pages of one of them, but that was sufficient. And then that professional world of bogus artists and bogus writers which he himself frequents. No wonder he wants to escape from it once in a while, and meet an occasional duchess. Men like him always feel they have missed something. You can leave the arts alone, but it is very dangerous to play tricks with them. After all, you yourself tell me he has agreed to write an introduction to the work of Isbister—and then you ask me why I consider St. John Clarke leads a dull life."

"But will this new move make his life any better?"

"Why not?"

"He must always have been picture-blind."

"Some of my best patrons are that. Don't be so idealistic."

"But if you are not really interested in pictures, liking a Bonnard doesn't make you any happier than liking a Bouguereau."

"The act of conversion does, though."

"Besides, this will open up a new, much more lively world of social life. One must admit that."

"Of course."

"You are probably right."

Perhaps it was surprising that nothing of the kind had happened earlier, because St. John Clarke had employed a whole dynasty of secretaries before Members. But former secretaries had been expected to work hard in the background, rather than to exist as an important element in the household. Members had built up the post to something far more influential than anything achieved by those who had gone before him. The fact was that, as St. John Clarke grew older, he wrote less, while his desire to cut a social figure gained in volume. He began to require a secretary who was something more than a subordinate to answer the telephone and remember the date of invitations. It was natural enough that St. John Clarke, who was unmarried, should wish to delegate power in his establishment, and rely on someone to help him plan his daily life. He was fortunate in finding a young man so well equipped for the job; for even those who did not much care for Members personally had to admit that his methods, often erratic, were on the whole admirably suited to the life St. John Clarke liked to lead.

"Nothing equivocal about the position of Members in that *ménage*, do you think?" said Barnby.

"Not in the least."

"I don't think St. John Clarke is interested in either sex," said Barnby. "He fell in love with himself at first sight and it is a passion to which he has always remained faithful."

"Self-love seems so often unrequited."

"But not in the case of St. John Clarke," said Barnby. "He is entirely capable of getting along without what most of the rest of us need."

I had often heard that particular question discussed. Although his novels not uncommonly dealt with the in-

tricate problems of married life, St. John Clarke did not, in general, greatly care for the society of women, except that of ladies in a position to invite him to agreeable dinners and week-end parties. Such hospitality was, after all, no more than a small and fitting return for the labours of a lifetime, and one that few but the envious would have begrudged him. However, this lack of interest in the opposite sex had from time to time given rise to gossip. Those persons who make a hobby, even a kind of duty, of tracking down malicious whispers to their source were forced to report in the case of St. John Clarke that nothing in the smallest degree reprobate could be confirmed. This did not prevent the circulation of a certain amount of rather spiteful badinage on the subject of his secretary. Members was impervious to any such innuendo, perhaps even encouraging it to screen his own affairs with women. St. John Clarke, indifferent to this indulgence himself, naturally disapproved of an irregular life in others: especially in someone at such close quarters.

"So there he goes," said Barnby. "Head-first into the contemporary world."

He hunched his shoulders, and made a grimace, as if to express the violence, even agony, that had accompanied St. John Clarke's æsthetic metamorphosis. By easy stages we moved off to dinner at Foppa's.

TWO

A year or more later Isbister died. He had been in bad health for some little time, and caught pneumonia during a period of convalescence. The question of the introduction, pigeon-holed indefinitely, since St. John Clarke utterly refused to answer letters on the subject, was now brought into the light again by the obituaries. Little or no general news was about at the time, so these notices were fuller than might have been expected. One of them called Isbister "the British Franz Hals." There were photographs of him, with his Van Dyck beard and Inverness cape, walking with Mrs. Isbister, a former model, the "Morwenna" of many of his subjects. This was clearly the occasion to make another effort to complete and publish *The Art of Horace Isbister*. Artists, especially academic artists, can pass quickly into the shadows: forgotten as if they had never been.

Almost as a last resort, therefore, it had been arranged that I should meet Mark Members out of office hours, and talk things over "as man to man." For this assignation Members had chosen—of all places—the Ritz. Since becoming St. John Clarke's secretary he had acquired a taste for rich surroundings. It was that prolonged, flat, cheerless week that follows Christmas. My own existence seemed infinitely stagnant, relieved only by work on another book. Those interminable latter days of the dying year create an interval, as it were, of moral suspension: one form of life already passed away before another has had time to assert

some new, endemic characteristic. Imminent change of direction is for some reason often foreshadowed by such colourless patches of time.

Along Piccadilly a north wind was blowing down the side streets, roaring hoarsely for a minute or two at a time, then dropping suddenly into silence; and again, after a brief pause, beginning to roar once more, as if perpetually raging against the inconsistency of human conduct. The arches of the portico gave some shelter from this hurricane, at the same time forming a sort of antechamber leading on one side, through lighted glass, into another, milder country, where struggle against the forces of nature was at least less explicit than on the pavements. Outside was the northern winter; here among the palms the climate was almost tropical.

Although a Saturday evening, the place was crowded. A suggestion of life in warmer cities, far away from London, was increased by the presence of a large party of South Americans camped out not far from where I found a seat at one of the grey marble-topped tables. They were grouped picturesquely beneath the figure of the bronze nymph perched in her grotto of artificial rocks and fresh green ferns, a large family spreading over three or four of the tables while they chatted amicably with one another. There were swarthy young men with blue chins and pretty girls in smart frocks, the latter descending in point of age to mere children with big black eyes and brightly coloured bows in their hair. A bald, neat, elderly man, the rosette of some order in his buttonhole, his grey moustache closely clipped, discoursed gravely with two enormously animated ladies, both getting a shade plump in their black dresses.

Away on her pinnacle, the nymph seemed at once a member of this Latin family party, and yet at the same time morally separate from them: an English girl, perhaps,

staying with relations possessing business interests in South America, herself in love for the first time after a visit to some neighbouring estancia. Now she had strayed away from her hosts to enjoy delicious private thoughts in peace while she examined the grimacing face of the river-god carved in stone on the short surface of wall by the grotto. Pensive, quite unaware of the young tritons violently attempting to waft her away from the fountain by sounding their conches at full blast, she gazed full of wonder that no crystal stream gushed from the water-god's contorted jaws. Perhaps in such a place she expected a torrent of champagne. Although stark naked, the nymph looked immensely respectable; less provocative, indeed, than some of the fully dressed young women seated below her, whose olive skins and silk stockings helped to complete this most unwintry scene.

Waiting for someone in a public place develops a sense of individual loneliness, so that amongst all this pale pink and sage green furniture, under decorations of rich cream and dull gold, I felt myself cut off from the rest of the world. I began to brood on the complexity of writing a novel about English life, a subject difficult enough to handle with authenticity even of a crudely naturalistic sort, even more to convey the inner truth of the things observed. Those South Americans sitting opposite, coming from a Continent I had never visited, regarding which I possessed only the most superficial scraps of information, seemed in some respects easier to conceive in terms of a novel than most of the English people sitting round the room. Intricacies of social life make English habits unyielding to simplification, while understatement and irony —in which all classes of this island converse—upset the normal emphasis of reported speech.

How, I asked myself, could a writer attempt to describe

in a novel such a young man as Mark Members, for example, possessing so much in common with myself, yet so different? How could this difference be expressed to that grave middle-aged South American gentleman talking to the plump ladies in black? Viewed from some distance off, Members and I might reasonably be considered almost identical units of the same organism, scarcely to be differentiated even by the sociological expert. We were both about the same age, had been to the same university, and were committed to the same profession of literature; though Members could certainly claim in that sphere a more notable place than myself, having by then published several books of poems and made some name for himself as a critic.

Thinking about Members that evening, I found myself unable to consider him without prejudice. He had been, I now realised, responsible for preventing St. John Clarke from writing the Isbister introduction. That was in itself understandable. However, he had also prevaricated about the matter in a way that showed disregard for the fact that we had known each other for a long time; and had always got along together pretty well. There were undoubtedly difficulties on his side too. Prejudice was to be avoided if— as I had idly pictured him—Members were to form the basis of a character in a novel. Alternatively, prejudice might prove the very element through which to capture and pin down unequivocally the otherwise elusive nature of what was of interest, discarding by its selective power the empty, unprofitable shell making up that side of Members untranslatable into terms of art; concentrating his final essence, his position, as it were, in eternity, into the medium of words.

Any but the most crude indication of my own personality would be, I reflected, equally hard to transcribe; at any

rate one that did not sound a little absurd. It was all very
well for Mrs. Erdleigh to generalise; far less easy to take
an objective view oneself. Even the bare facts had an unreal, almost satirical ring when committed to paper, say in
the manner of innumerable Russian stories of the nine-
teenth century: " I was born in the city of L——, the
son of an infantry officer . . ." To convey much that was
relevant to the reader's mind by such phrases was in this
country hardly possible. Too many factors had to be taken
into consideration. Understatement, too, had its own
banality; for, skirting cheap romanticism, it could also
encourage evasion of unpalatable facts.

However, these meditations on writing were dispersed by
the South Americans, who now rose in a body, and, with
a good deal of talking and shrill laughter, trooped down
the steps, making for the Arlington Street entrance. Their
removal perceptibly thinned the population of the palm
court. Among a sea of countenances, stamped like the skin
of Renoir's women with that curiously pink, silky surface
that seems to come from prolonged sitting about in Ritz
hotels, I noticed several familiar faces. Some of these belonged to girls once encountered at dances, now no longer
known, probably married; moving at any rate in circles
I did not frequent.

Margaret Budd was there, with a lady who looked like
an aunt or mother-in-law. In the end this " beauty " had
married a Scotch landowner, a husband rather older than
might have been expected for such a lovely girl. He was
in the whisky business, said to be hypochondriacal and bad-
tempered. Although by then mother of at least two children, Margaret still looked like one of those golden-haired,
blue-eyed dolls which say, " Ma-ma " and " Pa-Pa," closing
their eyes when tilted backward: unchanged in her possession of that peculiarly English beauty, scarcely to be

altered by grey hair or the pallor of age. Not far from her, on one of the sofas, sandwiched between two men, both of whom had the air of being rather rich, sat a tall, blonde young woman I recognised as Lady Ardglass, popularly supposed to have been for a short time mistress of Prince Theodoric. Unlike Margaret Budd—whose married name I could not remember—Bijou Ardglass appeared distinctly older : more than a little ravaged by the demands of her strenuous existence. She had lost some of that gay, energetic air of being ready for anything which she had so abundantly possessed when I had first seen her at Mrs. Andriadis's party. That occasion seemed an eternity ago.

As time passed, people leaving, others arriving, I began increasingly to suspect that Members was not going to show up. That would not be out of character, because cutting appointments was a recognised element in his method of conducting life. This habit—to be in general associated with a strong, sometimes frustrated desire to impose the will—is usually attributed on each specific occasion to the fact that " something better turned up." Such defaulters are almost as a matter of course reproached with trying to make a more profitable use of their time. Perhaps, in reality, self-interest in its crudest form plays less part in these deviations than might be supposed. The manœuvre may often be undertaken for its own sake. The person awaited deliberately withholds himself from the person awaiting. Mere absence is in this manner turned into a form of action, even potentially violent in its consequences. Possibly Members, from an inner compulsion, had suddenly decided to establish ascendancy by such an assertion of the will. On the other hand, the action would in the circumstances represent such an infinitesimal score against life in general that his absence, if deliberate, was probably attributable to some minor move in domestic politics vis-à-

vis St. John Clarke. I was thinking over these possibilities, rather gloomily wondering whether or not I would withdraw or stay a few minutes longer, when an immensely familiar head and shoulders became visible for a second through a kind of window, or embrasure, looking out from the palm court on to the lower levels of the passage and rooms beyond. It was Peter Templer. A moment later he strolled up the steps.

For a few seconds Templer gazed thoughtfully round the room, as if contemplating the deterioration of a landscape, known from youth, once famed for its natural beauty, now ruined beyond recall. He was about to turn away, when he caught sight of me and came towards the table. It must have been at least three years since we had met. His sleekly brushed hair and long, rather elegant stride were just the same. His face was perhaps a shade fuller, and his eyes at once began to give out that familiar blue mechanical sparkle that I remembered so well from our schooldays. With a red carnation in the buttonhole of his dark suit, his shirt cuffs cut tightly round the wrist so that somehow his links asserted themselves unduly, Templer's air was distinctly prosperous. But he also looked as if by then he knew what worry was, something certainly unknown to him in the past.

" I suppose you are waiting for someone, Nick," he said, drawing up a chair. " Some ripe little piece?"

" You're very wide of the mark."

"Then a dowager is going to buy your dinner—after which she will make you an offer?"

"No such luck."

" What then?"

" I'm waiting for a man."

" I say, old boy, sorry to have been so inquisitive. Things have come to that, have they?"

" You couldn't know."

" I should have guessed."

" Have a drink, anyway."

I remembered reading, some years before, an obituary notice in the *Morning Post*, referring to his father's death. This paragraph, signed " A.S.F.," was, in fact, a brief personal memoir rather than a bald account of the late Mr. Templer's career. Although the deceased's chairmanship of various companies was mentioned—his financial interests had been chiefly in cement—more emphasis was laid on his delight in sport, especially boxing, his many undisclosed benefactions to charity, the kind heart within him, always cloaked by a deceptively brusque manner. The initials, together with a certain banality of phrasing, suggested the hand of Sunny Farebrother, Mr. Templer's younger City associate I had met at their house. That visit had been the sole occasion when I had seen Templer's father. I had wondered vaguely—to use a favourite expression of his son's—" how much he had cut up for." Details about money are always of interest; even so, I did not give the matter much thought. Already I had begun to think of Peter Templer as a friend of my schooldays rather than one connected with that more recent period of occasional luncheons together, during the year following my own establishment in London after coming down from the university. When, once in a way, I had attended the annual dinner for members of Le Bas's House, Templer had never been present.

That we had ceased to meet fairly regularly was due no doubt to some extent to Templer's chronic inability—as our housemaster Le Bas would have said—to " keep up " a friendship. He moved entirely within the orbit of events of the moment, looking neither forward nor backward. If we happened to run across each other, we arranged to do

something together; not otherwise. This mutual detachment had been brought about also by the circumstances of my own life. To be circumscribed by people constituting the same professional community as myself was no wish of mine; rather the contrary. However, an inexorable law governs all human existence in that respect, ordaining that sooner or later everyone must appear before the world as he is. Many are not prepared to face this sometimes distasteful principle. Indeed, the illusion that anyone can escape from the marks of his vocation is an aspect of romanticism common to every profession; those occupied with the world of action claiming their true interests to lie in the pleasure of imagination or reflection, while persons principally concerned with reflective or imaginative pursuits are for ever asserting their inalienable right to participation in an active sphere.

Perhaps Templer himself lay somewhere within the range of this definition. If so, he gave little indication of it. In fact, if taxed, there can be no doubt that he would have denied any such thing. The outward sign that seemed to place him within this category was his own unwillingness ever wholly to accept the people amongst whom he had chosen to live. A curious streak of melancholy seemed to link him with a less arid manner of life than that to which he seemed irrevocably committed. At least I supposed something of that sort could still be said of his life; for I knew little or nothing of his daily routine, in or out of the office, though suspecting that neither his activities, nor his friends, were of a kind likely to be very sympathetic to myself.

However, various strands, controlled without much method and then invisible to me, imparted a certain irregular pattern to Templer's personal affairs. For example, he liked his friends to be rich and engrossed in whatever

business occupied them. They had to be serious about money, though relatively dissipated in their private lives; to possess no social ambitions whatever, though at the same time to be disfigured by no grave social defects. The women had to be good-looking, the men tolerably proficient at golf and bridge, without making a fetish of those pastimes. Both sexes, when entertained by him, were expected to drink fairly heavily; although, here again, intoxication must not be carried to excess. In fact, broadly speaking, Templer disliked anything that could be labelled "bohemian," as much as anything with claims to be "smart." He did not fancy even that sort of "smartness" to be found to a limited extent in the City, a form of life which had, after all, so much in common with his own tastes.

"You know, I really rather hate the well-born," he used to say. "Not that I see many of them these days."

Nothing might be thought easier than gratification of these modest requirements among a circle of intimates; and the difficulty Templer found in settling down to any one set of persons limited by these terms of reference, and at the same time satisfactory to himself, was really remarkable. This side of him suggested a kind of "spoiled intellectual." There was also the curious sympathy he could extend to such matters as the story of the St. John Clarke introduction, which he now made me outline after I had explained my purpose in the Ritz. The facts could scarcely have been very interesting to him, but he followed their detail as if alteration of the bank rate or fluctuations of the copper market were ultimately concerned. Perhaps this capacity for careful attention to other people's affairs was the basis of his own success in business.

"Of course I know about Isbister, R.A.," he said. "He painted that shocking picture of my old man. I tried to

pop it when he dropped off the hooks, but there were no takers. I know about St. John Clarke, too. Mona reads his books. Absolutely laps them up, in fact."

" Who is Mona?"

" Oh, yes, you haven't met her yet, have you? Mona is my wife."

" But, my dear Peter, I had no idea you were married."

" Strange, isn't it? Our wedding anniversary, matter of fact. Broke as I am, I thought we could gnaw a cutlet at the Grill to celebrate. Why not join us? Your chap is obviously not going to turn up."

He began to speak of his own affairs, talking in just the way he did when we used to have tea together at school. Complaining of having lost a lot of money in " the slump," he explained that he still owned a house in the neighbourhood of Maidenhead.

" More or less camping out there now," he said. " With a married couple looking after us. The woman does the cooking. The man can drive a car and service it pretty well, but he hasn't the foggiest idea about looking after my clothes."

I asked about his marriage.

" We met first at a road-house near Staines. Mona was being entertained there by a somewhat uncouth individual called Snider, an advertising agent. Snider's firm was using her as a photographer's model. You'll know her face when you see her. Laxatives—halitosis—even her closest friend wouldn't tell her—and so on."

I discovered in due course that Mona's chief appearance on the posters had been to advertise toothpaste; but both she and her husband were inclined to emphasise other more picturesque possibilities.

" She'd already had a fairly adventurous career by then," Templer said.

He began to enlarge on this last piece of information, like a man unable to forgo irritating the quiescent nerve of a potentially aching tooth. I had the impression that he was still very much in love with his wife, but that things were perhaps not going as well as he could wish. That would explain a jerkiness of manner that suggested worry. The story itself seemed commonplace enough, yet containing implications of Templer's own recurrent desire to escape from whatever world enclosed him.

" She *says* she's partly Swiss," he said. " Her father was an engineer in Birmingham, always being fired for being tight. However, both parents are dead. The only relation she's got is an aunt with a house in Worthing—a boarding-house, I think."

I saw at once that Mona, whatever else her characteristics, was a wife liberally absolving Templer from additional family ties. That fact, perhaps counting for little compared with deeper considerations, would at the same time seem a great advantage in his eyes. This desire to avoid new relations through marriage was connected with an innate unwillingness to identify himself too closely with any one social group. In that taste, oddly enough, he resembled Uncle Giles, each of them considering himself master of a more sweeping mobility of action by voluntary withdrawal from competition at any given social level of existence.

At the time of narration, I did not inwardly accept all Templer's highly coloured statements about his wife, but I was impressed by the apparent depths of his feeling for Mona. Even when telling the story of how his marriage had come about, he had completely abandoned any claim to have employed those high-handed methods he was accustomed to advocate for handling girls of her sort. I asked what time she was due at the Ritz.

"When she comes out of the cinema," he said. "She was determined to see *Mädchen in Uniform*. I couldn't face it. After all, one meets quite enough lesbians in real life without going to the pictures to see them."

"But it isn't a film about lesbians."

"Oh, isn't it?" said Templer. "Mona thought it was. She'll be disappointed if you're right. However, I'm sure you're wrong. Jimmy Brent told me about it. He usually knows what's what in matters of that kind. My sister Jean is with Mona. Did you ever meet her? I can't remember. They may be a little late, but I've booked a table. We can have a drink or two while we wait."

Jean's name recalled the last time I had seen her at that luncheon party at Stourwater where I had been taken by the Walpole-Wilsons. I had not thought of her for ages, though some small residue of inner dissatisfaction, that survives all emotional expenditure come to nothing, now returned.

"Jean's having a spot of trouble with that husband of hers," said Templer. "That is why she is staying with us for the moment. She married Bob Duport, you know. He is rather a handful."

"So I should imagine."

"You don't know him."

"We met when you drove us all into the ditch in your famous second-hand Vauxhall."

"My God," said Templer, laughing. "That was a shambles, wasn't it? Fancy your remembering that. It must be nearly ten years ago now. The row those bloody girls made. Old Bob was in poor form that day, I remember. He thought he'd picked up a nail after a binge he'd been on a night or two before. Completely false alarm, of course."

" As Le Bas once said : ' I can't accept ill health as a valid excuse for ill manners '."

" Bob's not much your sort, but he's not a bad chap when you get to know him. I was surprised you'd ever heard of him. I've had worse brothers-in-law, although, God knows, that's not saying much. But Bob *is* difficult. Bad enough running after every girl he meets, but when he goes and loses nearly all his money on top of that, an awkward situation is immediately created."

" Are they living apart?"

" Not officially. Jean is looking for a small flat in town for herself and the kid."

" What sex?"

" Polly, aged three."

" And Duport?"

" Gone abroad, leaving a trail of girl-friends and bad debts behind him. He is trying to put through some big stuff on the metal market. I think the two of them will make it up in due course. I used to think she was mad about him, but you can never tell with women."

The news that Polly was to be born was the last I had heard of her mother. Little as I could imagine how Jean had brought herself to marry Duport—far less be " mad about him "—I had by then learnt that such often inexplicable things must simply be accepted as matters of fact. His sister's matrimonial troubles evidently impressed Templer as vexatious, though in the circumstances probably unavoidable; certainly not a subject for prolonged discussion.

" Talking of divorces and such things," he said. " Do you ever see Charles Stringham now?"

There had been little or no scandal connected with the break-up of Stringham's marriage. He and Peggy Stepney had parted company without apparent reason, just as their reason for marrying had been outwardly hard to under-

stand. They had bought a house somewhere north of the Park, but neither ever seemed to have lived there for more than a few weeks at a time, certainly seldom together. The house itself, decorated by the approved decorator of that moment, was well spoken of, but I had never been there. The marriage had simply collapsed, so people said, from inanition. I never heard it suggested that Peggy had taken a lover. Stringham, it was true, was seen about with all kinds of women, though nothing specific was alleged against him either. Soon after the decree had been made absolute, Peggy married a cousin, rather older than herself, and went to live in Yorkshire, where her husband possessed a large house, noted in books of authentically recorded ghost stories for being rather badly haunted.

" That former wife of his—The Lady Peggy—was a good-looking piece," said Templer. " But, as you know, such grand life is not for me. I prefer simpler pleasures——

" ' Oh, give me a man to whom naught comes amiss,
     One horse or another, that country or this. . . . ' "

" You know you've always hated hunting and hunting people. Anyway, whose sentiments were those?"

" Ah," he said, " chaps like you think I'm not properly educated, in spite of the efforts of Le Bas and others, and that I don't know about beautiful poetry. You find you're wrong. I know all sorts of little snatches. As a matter of fact I was thinking of women, really, rather than horses, and taking 'em as you find 'em. Not being too choosy about it as Charles has always been. Of course they are easier to take than to find, in my experience—though of course it is not gentlemanly to boast of such things. Anyway, as you know, I have given up all that now."

At school I could remember Templer claiming that he

had never read a book for pleasure in his life; and, although an occasional Edgar Wallace was certainly to be seen in his hand during the period of his last few terms, the quotation was surprising. That was a side of him not entirely unexpected, but usually kept hidden. Incidentally, it was a conversational trick acquired—perhaps consciously copied—from Stringham.

"You remember the imitations Charles used to do of Widmerpool?" he said. "I expect he is much too grand to remember Widmerpool now."

"I saw Widmerpool not so long ago. He is with Donners-Brebner."

"But not much longer," said Templer. "Widmerpool is joining the Acceptance World."

"What on earth is that?"

"Well, actually he is going to become a bill-broker," said Templer, laughing. "I should have made myself clearer to one not involved in the nefarious ways of the City."

"What will he do?"

"Make a lot of heavy weather. He'll have to finish his lunch by two o'clock and spend the rest of the day wasting the time of the banks."

"But what is the Acceptance World?"

"If you have goods you want to sell to a firm in Bolivia, you probably do not touch your money in the ordinary way until the stuff arrives there. Certain houses, therefore, are prepared to ' accept ' the debt. They will advance you the money on the strength of your reputation. It is all right when the going is good, but sooner or later you are tempted to plunge. Then there is an alteration in the value of the Bolivian exchange, or a revolution, or perhaps the firm just goes bust—and you find yourself stung. That is, if you guess wrong."

"I see. But why is he leaving Donners-Brebner? He always told me he was such a success there and that Sir Magnus liked him so much."

"Widmerpool was doing all right in Donners-Brebner—in fact rather well, as you say," said Templer. "But he used to bore the pants off everyone in the combine by his intriguing. In the end he got on the nerves of Donners himself. Did you ever come across a fellow called Truscott? Widmerpool took against him, and worked away until he had got him out. Then Donners regretted it, after Truscott had been sacked, and decided Widmerpool was getting too big for his boots. He must go too. The long and the short of it is that Widmerpool is joining this firm of bill-brokers—on the understanding that a good deal of the Donners-Brebner custom follows him there."

I had never before heard Templer speak of Widmerpool in this matter-of-fact way. At school he had disliked him, or, at best, treated him as a harmless figure of fun. Now, however, Widmerpool had clearly crystallised in Templer's mind as an ordinary City acquaintance, to be thought of no longer as a subject for laughter, but as a normal vehicle for the transaction of business; perhaps even one particularly useful in that respect on account of former associations.

"I was trying to get Widmerpool to lend a hand with old Bob," said Templer.

"What would he do?"

"Bob has evolved a scheme for collecting scrap metal from some place in the Balkans and shipping it home. At least that is the simplest way of explaining what he intends. Widmerpool has said he will try to arrange for Bob to have the agency for Donners-Brebner."

I was more interested in hearing of this development in Widmerpool's career than in examining its probable effect on Duport, whose business worries were no concern of

mine. However, my attention was at that moment distracted from such matters by the sudden appearance in the palm court of a short, decidedly unconventional figure who now came haltingly up the steps. This person wore a black leather overcoat. His arrival in the Ritz—in those days—was a remarkable event.

Pausing, with a slight gesture of exhaustion that seemed to imply arduous travel over many miles of arid desert or snowy waste (according to whether the climate within or without the hotel was accepted as prevailing), he looked about the room; gazing as if in amazement at the fountain, the nymph, the palms in their pots of Chinese design: then turning his eyes to the chandeliers and the glass of the roof. His bearing was at once furtive, resentful, sagacious, and full of a kind of confidence in his own powers. He seemed to be surveying the tables as if searching for someone, at the same time unable to believe his eyes, while he did so, at the luxuriance of the oasis in which he found himself. He carried no hat, but retained the belted leather overcoat upon which a few drops of moisture could be seen glistening as he advanced farther into the room, an indication that snow or sleet had begun to fall outside. This black leather garment gave a somewhat official air to his appearance, obscurely suggesting a Wellsian man of the future, hierarchic in rank. Signs of damp could also be seen in patches on his sparse fair hair, a thatch failing to roof in completely the dry, yellowish skin of his scalp.

This young man, although already hard to think of as really young on account of the maturity of his expression, was J. G. Quiggin. I had been reflecting on him only a short time earlier in connection with Mark Members; for the pair of them—Members and Quiggin—were, for some reason, always associated together in the mind. This was not only because I myself had happened to meet both of

them during my first term at the university. Other people, too, were accustomed to link their names together, as if they were a business firm, or, more authentically, a couple whose appearance together in public inevitably invoked the thought of a certain sort of literary life. Besides that, a kind of love-hate indissolubly connected them.

Whether or not the birth of this relationship had in fact taken place at that tea party in Sillery's rooms in college, where we had all met as freshmen, was not easy to say. There at any rate I had first seen Quiggin in his grubby starched collar and subfusc suit. On that occasion Sillery had rather maliciously suggested the acquaintance of Members and Quiggin dated from an earlier incarnation; in fact boyhood together—like Isbister and St. John Clarke —in some Midland town. So far as I knew, that assertion had neither been proved nor disproved. Some swore Quiggin and Members were neighbours at home; others that the story was a pure invention, produced in malice, and based on the fact that Sillery had found the two names in the same provincial telephone directory. Sillery certainly devoted a good deal of his time to the study of such works of reference as telephone books and county directories, from which he managed to extract a modicum of information useful to himself. At the same time there were those who firmly believed Members and Quiggin to be related; even first cousins. The question was largely irrelevant; although the acutely combative nature of their friendship, if it could be so called, certainly possessed all that intense, almost vindictive rivalry of kinship.

Quiggin had quietly disappeared from the university without taking a degree. Now, like Members, he had already made some name for himself, though at a somewhat different literary level. He was a professional reviewer of notable ability, much disliked by some of the older critics

for the roughness with which he occasionally handled accepted reputations. One of the smaller publishing houses employed him as "literary adviser;" a firm of which his friend Howard Craggs (formerly of the Vox Populi Press, now extinct, though partly reincorporated as Boggis & Stone) had recently become a director. A book by Quiggin had been advertised to appear in the spring, but as a rule his works never seemed, at the last moment, to satisfy their author's high standard of self-criticism. Up to then his manuscripts had always been reported as "burnt," or at best held back for drastic revision.

Quiggin, certainly to himself and his associates, represented a more go-ahead school of thought to that of Members and his circle. Although not himself a poet, he was a great adherent of the new trends of poetry then developing, which deprecated "Art for Art's sake," a doctrine in a general way propagated by Members. However, Members, too, was moving with the times, his latest volume of verse showing a concern with psychoanalysis; but, although "modern" in the eyes of a writer of an older generation like St. John Clarke, Members—so Quiggin had once remarked—"drooped too heavily over the past, a crutch with which we younger writers must learn to dispense." Members, for his part, had been heard complaining that he himself was in sympathy with "all liberal and progressive movements," but "J. G. had advanced into a state of mind too political to be understood by civilised people." In spite of such differences, and reported statements of both of them that they "rarely saw each other now," they were not uncommonly to be found together, arguing or sulking on the banquettes of the Café Royal.

When Quiggin caught sight of me in the Ritz he immediately made for our table. As he moved across the white marble floor his figure seemed thicker than formerly.

From being the spare, hungry personage I had known as an undergraduate he had become solid, almost stout. It was possible that Members, perhaps maliciously, perhaps as a matter of convenience to himself, had arranged for Quiggin to pick him up for dinner at an hour when our business together would be at an end. Supposing this had been planned, I was preparing to explain that Members had not turned up, when all at once Quiggin himself began to speak in his small, hard, grating North Country voice; employing a tone very definitely intended to sweep aside any question of wasting time upon the idle formalities of introduction, or indeed anything else that might postpone, even momentarily, some matter that was his duty to proclaim without delay.

"I could not get away earlier," he began, peremptorily. "St. J. is rather seriously ill. It happened quite suddenly. Not only that, but a difficult situation has arisen. I should like to discuss things with you."

This introductory speech was even less expected than Quiggin's own arrival, although the tense, angry seriousness with which he had invested these words was not uncommon in his way of talking. Once I had thought this abrupt, aggressive manner came from a kind of shyness; but later that theory had to be abandoned when it became clear that Quiggin's personality expressed itself naturally in this form. I was surprised to hear him refer to St. John Clarke as " St. J.," a designation appropriated to himself by Mark Members, and rarely used by others; in fact a nickname almost patented by Members as an outward sign of his own intimacy with his friend and employer.

I could not imagine why Quiggin, on that particular night, should suddenly wish that we should dine *tête-à-tête*. In the past we had occasionally spent an evening together after meeting at some party, always by accident

rather than design. We were on quite good terms, but there was no subject involving St. John Clarke likely to require urgent discussion between us. At the university, where he had seemed a lonely, out-of-the-way figure, I had felt an odd interest in Quiggin; but our acquaintance there, such as it was, he now treated almost as a matter to live down. Perhaps that was natural as he came to invest more and more of his personality in his own literary status. At that moment, for example, his manner of speaking implied that any of his friends should be prepared to make sacrifices for an exceptional occasion like this one: a time when opportunity to be alone with him and talk seriously was freely offered.

" Did you come to meet Mark?" I asked. " He hasn't turned up. It is not very likely he will appear now."

Quiggin, refusing an invitation to sit down, stood upright by the table, still enveloped in his black, shiny livery. He had unfastened the large buttons of the overcoat, which now flapped open like Bonaparte's revealing a dark grey jumper that covered all but the knot of a red tie. The shirt was also dark grey. His face wore the set, mask-like expression of an importunate beggar tormenting a pair of tourists seated on the perimeter of a café's *terrasse*. I felt suddenly determined to be no longer a victim of other people's disregard for their social obligations. I introduced Templer out of hand—an operation Quiggin had somehow prevented until that moment—explaining at the same time that I was that evening already irrevocably booked for a meal.

Quiggin showed annoyance at this downright refusal to be dislodged, simultaneously indicating his own awareness that Members had been unable to keep this appointment. It then occurred to me that Members had persuaded Quiggin to make the excuses for his own absence in person.

Such an arrangement was unlikely, and would in any case not explain why Quiggin should expect me to dine with him. However, Quiggin shook his head at this suggestion, and gave a laugh—expressing scorn rather than amusement. Templer watched us with interest.

"As a matter of fact St. J. has a new secretary," said Quiggin slowly, through closed lips. "That is why Mark did not come this evening.

"What, has Mark been sacked?"

Quiggin was evidently not prepared to reply directly to so uncompromising an enquiry. He laughed a little, though rather more leniently than before.

"Honourably retired, perhaps one might say."

"On a pension?"

"You are very inquisitive, Nicholas."

"You have aroused my interest. You should be flattered."

"Life with St. J. never really gave Mark time for his own work."

"He always produced a fair amount."

"Too much, from one point of view," said Quiggin, savagely; adding in a less severe tone: "Mark, as you know, always insists on taking on so many things. He could not always give St. J. the attention a man of his standing quite reasonably demands. Of course, the two of them will continue to see each other. I think, in fact, Mark is going to look in once in a way to keep the library in order. After all, they are close friends, first and foremost, quite apart from whether or not Mark is St. J.'s secretary. As you probably know, there have been various difficulties from time to time. Minor ones, of course. Still, one thing leads to another. Mark can be rather querulous when he does not get his own way."

" Who is taking Mark's place?"

" It is not exactly a question of one person taking another's place. Merely coping with the practical side of the job more—well—conscientiously."

Quiggin bared his teeth, as if to excuse this descent on his own part to a certain smugness of standpoint.

" Yourself?"

" At first just as an experiment on both sides."

I saw at once that in this change, if truly reported, all kind of implications were inherent. Stories had circulated in the past of jobs for which Quiggin and Members had been in competition, most of them comparatively unimportant employments in the journalistic field. This was rather larger game; because, apart from other considerations, there was the question of who was to be St. John Clarke's heir. He was apparently alone in the world. It was not a vast fortune, perhaps, but a tidy sum. A devoted secretary might stand in a favourable position for at least a handsome bequest. Although I had never heard hints that Quiggin was anxious to replace Members in the novelist's household, such an ambition was by no means unthinkable. In fact the change was likely to have been brought about by long intrigue rather than sudden caprice. The news was surprising, though of a kind to startle by its essential appropriateness rather than from any sense of incongruity. Although I did not know St. John Clarke, I could not help feeling a certain pity for him, smitten down among his first editions, press cuttings, dinner invitations, and signed photographs of eminent contemporaries, a sick man of letters, fought over by Members and Quiggin.

" That was why I wanted to have a talk about St. J.'s affairs," said Quiggin, continuing to speak in his more conciliatory tone. " There have been certain changes lately

in his point of view. You probably knew that. I think you are interested in getting this introduction. I see no reason why he should not write it. But I am of the opinion that he will probably wish to approach Isbister's painting from a rather different angle. The pictures, after all, offer a unique example of what a capitalist society produces where art is concerned. However, I see we shall have to discuss that another time."

He stared hard at Templer as chief impediment to his plans for the evening. It was at that point that " the girls " arrived; owing to this conversation, entering the room unobserved by me until they were standing beside us. I was immediately aware that I had seen Templer's wife before. Then I remembered that he had warned me I should recognise the stylised, conventionally smiling countenance, set in blonde curls, that had formerly appeared so often, on the walls of buses and underground trains, advocating a well-known brand of toothpaste. She must have been nearly six foot in height: in spite of a rather coarse complexion, a beautiful girl by any standards.

" It was *too* wonderful," she said, breathlessly.

She spoke to Templer, but turned almost at once in the direction of Quiggin and myself. At the sight of her, Quiggin went rather red in the face and muttered inaudible phrases conveying that they already knew one another. She replied civilly to these, though evidently without any certainty as to where that supposed meeting had taken place. She was obviously longing to talk about the film, but Quiggin was not prepared for the matter of their earlier encounter to be left vague.

" It was years ago at a party over an antique shop," he insisted, " given by an old queen who died soon after. Mark Members introduced us."

" Oh, yes," she said, indifferently, " I haven't seen Mark for ages."

" Deacon, he was called."

" I believe I remember."

" Off Charlotte Street."

" There were a lot of parties round there," she agreed.

Then I knew that something other than the toothpaste advertisements had caused Mona's face to seem so familiar. I, too, had seen her at Mr. Deacon's birthday party. Since then she had applied peroxide to her naturally dark hair. When Templer had spoken of his wife's former profession I had not connected her with " Mona," the artist's model of whom Barnby, and others, used sometimes to speak. Barnby had not mentioned her for a long time.

In due course I found that Mona had abandoned that " artist's " world for commercial employments that were more lucrative. The people she met in these less pretentious circles were also no doubt on the whole more sympathetic to her, although she would never have admitted that. Certainly the impact of her earlier career as a model for painters and sculptors was never erased from her own mind. With the extraordinary adaptability of women, she had managed to alter considerably the lines of her figure, formerly a striking synthesis of projections and concavities that certainly seemed to demand immediate expression in bronze or stone. Now her body had been disciplined into a fashionable, comparatively commonplace mould. She smiled in a friendly way at Quiggin, but made no effort to help him out in his efforts to suggest that they really already knew each other.

Quiggin himself continued to stand for a time resentfully beside us, giving the impression not so much that he wished to join the Templer party, as that he hoped for an in-

vitation to do so, which would at once be curtly refused;
whether, had the chance arisen, he would in fact have
withheld his company was, of course, speculative. Mona
threw him another smile, her regular rows of teeth neatly
displayed between pink lips parted in a cupid's bow:
an ensemble invoking more than ever her career on the
hoardings. For some reason this glance confirmed Quiggin's intention to depart. After a final word with me to
the effect that he would ring up early the following week
and arrange a meeting, he nodded in an offended manner
to the world in general, and tramped away across the room
and down the steps. He held himself tautly upright, as if
determined to avoid for ever in future such haunts of
luxury and those who frequent them.

Just as he was making this move, Lady Ardglass, followed by her spruce, grey-haired admirers, at heel like a
brace of well-groomed, well-bred, obedient sporting dogs,
passed us on the way out. A natural blonde, Bijou Ardglass possessed a fleeting facial resemblance to Mona. She
was said to have been a mannequin before her marriage.
My attention had been caught momentarily by Quiggin's
words, but, even while he was speaking, I was aware of
this resemblance as Lady Ardglass approached; although
her smooth hair and mink made a strong contrast with
Mona's camel-hair coat and rather wild appearance. All
the same there could be no doubt that the two of them possessed something in common. As the Ardglass cortège
came level with us, I saw exchanged between the two of
them one of those glances so characteristic of a woman
catching sight of another woman who reminds her of herself : glances in which deep hatred and also a kind of passionate love seem to mingle voluptuously together for an
instant of time.

Templer, at the same moment, shot out an all-embracing

look, which seemed in an equally brief space to absorb
Bijou Ardglass in her entirety. He appeared to do this
more from force of habit than because she greatly interested him. It was a memorandum for some future date,
should the need ever arise, recording qualities and defects,
charms and blemishes, certainties and potentialities, both
moral and physical. Jean saw Lady Ardglass too. Just as
Quiggin was making his final remark to me, I was conscious that she touched her brother's arm and muttered
something to him that sounded like " Bob's girl : " words at
which Templer raised his eyebrows.

I did not fully take in Jean's appearance until that
moment. She was wearing a red dress with a black coat,
and some kind of a scarf, folded over like a stock, emphasised the long, graceful curve of her neck. Mona's
strident personality occupied the centre of the stage, and,
besides, I felt for some reason a desire to postpone our
meeting. Now, as she spoke to her brother, her face assumed an expression at once mocking and resigned, which
had a sweetness about it that reminded me of the days
when I had thought myself in love with her. I could still
feel the tension her presence always brought, but without
any of that hopeless romantic longing, so characteristic of
love's very early encounters : perhaps always imperfectly
recaptured in the more realistic love-making of later life.
Now, I experienced a kind of resentment at the reserve
which enclosed her. It suggested a form of self-love, not
altogether attractive. Yet the look of irony and amusement
that had come into her face when she whispered the phrase
about " Bob's girl " seemed to add something unexpected
and charming to her still mysterious personality.

She was taller than I remembered, and carried herself
well. Her face, like her brother's, had become a shade
fuller, a change that had coarsened his appearance, while in

her the sharp, almost animal look I remembered was now softened. She had not entirely lost her air of being a school-girl; though certainly, it had to be admitted, a very smartly dressed school-girl. I thought to myself, not without complacence, that I was able to appreciate her without in any way losing my head, as I might once have done. There was still a curious fascination about her grey-blue eyes, slanting a little, as it were caught tightly between soft, lazy lids and dark, luxurious lashes. Once she had reminded me of Rubens's *Chapeau de Paille*. Now for some reason—though there was not much physical likeness between them—I thought of the woman smoking the hookah in Delacroix's *Femmes d'Alger dans leur appartement*. Perhaps there was something of the odalisque about Jean, too. She looked pale and rather tired. Any girl might excusably have appeared pale beside Mona, whose naturally high colouring had been increased by her own hand, almost as if for the stage or a cabaret performance.

" Do you remember where we last met?" she said, when Quiggin was gone.

" At Stourwater."

" What a party."

" Was it awful?"

" Some of it wasn't very nice. Terrible rows between Baby and our host."

" But I thought they never had rows in public."

" They didn't. That was what was so awful. Sir Magnus tremendously bland all the time and Baby absolutely bursting with bad temper."

" Do you ever hear from Baby Wentworth now?"

" I had a card at Christmas. She is cloudlessly happy with her Italian."

" What is his profession?"

"I don't think I know you well enough to tell you. Perhaps after dinner."

This, I remembered, was the way things had been at Stourwater: brisk conversation that led in the end to acres of silence. I made up my mind that this time I would not feel put out by her behaviour, whatever form it took.

"Let's have some food," said Templer, "I'm famished. So must you girls be, after your intellectual film."

Afterwards, I could never recall much about that dinner in the Grill, except that the meal conveyed an atmosphere of powerful forces at work beneath the conversation. The sight of her husband's mistress had no doubt been disturbing to Jean, who as usual spoke little. It soon became clear that the Templers' mutual relationship was not an easy one. Different couples approach with varied technique the matrimonial vehicle's infinitely complicated machinery. In the case of the Templers, their method made it hard to believe that they were really married at all. Clearly each of them was accustomed to a more temporary arrangement. Their conduct was normal enough, but they remained two entirely separate individuals, giving no indication of a life in common. This was certainly not because Templer showed any lack of interest in his wife. On the contrary, he seemed extravagantly, almost obsessively fond of her, although he teased her from time to time. In the past he had sometimes spoken of his love affairs to me, but I had never before seen him, as it were, in action. I wondered whether he habitually showed this same tremendous outward enthusiasm when pursuing more casual inclinations; or whether Mona had touched off some hitherto unkindled spark.

How far Mona herself reciprocated these feelings was less easy to guess. Possibly she was already rather bored

with being a wife, and her surfeit in this respect might explain her husband's conciliatory attitude. She spoke and acted in a manner so affected and absurd that there was something appealing about the artificiality of her gestures and conversation. She was like some savage creature, anxious to keep up appearances before members of a more highly civilised species, although at the same time keenly aware of her own superiority in cunning. There was something hard and untamed about her, probably the force that had attracted Templer and others. She seemed on good terms with Jean, who may have found her sister-in-law's crude, violent presence emphasised to advantage her own quieter, though still undisclosed nature.

Quiggin had made an impression upon Mona, because, almost immediately after we sat down to dinner, she began to make enquiries about him. Possibly, on thinking it over, she felt that his obvious interest in her had deserved greater notice. In answer to her questions, I explained that he was J. G. Quiggin, the literary critic. She at once asserted that she was familiar with his reviews in one of the " weeklies," mentioning, as it happened, a periodical for which, so far as I knew, he had never written.

" He was a splendid fellow in his old leather overcoat," said Templer. " Did you notice his shirt, too? I expect you know lots of people like that, Nick. To think I was rather worried at not having struggled into a dinner-jacket to-night, and he just breezed in wearing the flannel trousers he had been sleeping in for a fortnight, and not caring a damn. I admire that."

" I couldn't remember a thing about meeting him before," said Mona. " I expect I must have been a bit tight that night, otherwise I should have known his name. He said Mark Members introduced us. Have you heard of him? He is a well-known poet."

She said this with an ineffable silliness that was irresistible.

" I was going to meet him here, as a matter of fact, but he never turned up."

" Oh, *were* you?"

She was astonished at this; and impressed. I wondered what on earth Members had told her about himself to have won such respect in her eyes. Afterwards, I found that it was his status as " a poet," rather than his private personality, that made him of such interest to her.

" I never knew Mark well," she said, rather apologetic at having suggested such ambitious claims.

" He and Quiggin are usually very thick together."

" I didn't realise Nick was waiting for an old friend of yours, sweetie," said Templer. " Is he one of those fascinating people you sometimes tell me about, who wear beards and sandals and have such curious sexual habits?"

Mona began to protest, but Jean interrupted her by saying: " He's not a bad poet, is he?"

" I think rather good," I said, feeling a sudden unaccountable desire to encourage in her an interest in poetry. " He is St. John Clarke's secretary—or, least, he was."

I remembered then that, if Quiggin was to be believed, the situation between Members and St. John Clarke was a delicate one.

" I used to like St. John Clarke's novels," said Jean. " Now I think they are rather awful. Mona adores them."

" Oh, but they are *too* wonderful."

Mona began to detail some of St. John Clarke's plots, a formidable undertaking at the best of times. This expression of Jean's views—that Members was a goodish poet and St. John Clarke a bad novelist—seemed to me to indicate an impressive foothold in literary criticism. I felt now that I wanted to discuss all kind of things with her, but hardly

knew where to begin on account of the barrier she seemed to have set up between herself and the rest of the world. I suspected that she might merely be trying to veer away conversation from a period of Mona's life that would carry too many painful implications for Templer as a husband. It could be design, rather than literary interest. However, Mona herself was unwilling to be deflected from the subject.

" Do you run round with all those people?" she went on. " I used to myself. Then—oh, I don't know—I lost touch with them. Of course Peter doesn't much care for that sort of person, do you, sweetie?"

" Rubbish," said Templer. " I've just said how much I liked Mr. J. G. Quiggin. In fact I wish I could meet him again, and find out the name of his tailor."

Mona frowned at this refusal to take her remark seriously. She turned to me and said: " You know, you are not much like most of Peter's usual friends yourself."

That particular matter was all too complicated to explain, even if amenable to explanation, which I was inclined to doubt. I knew, of course, what she meant. Probably there was something to be said for accepting that opinion. The fact that I was not specially like the general run of Templer's friends had certainly been emphasised by the appearance of Quiggin. I was rather displeased that the Templers had seen Quiggin. To deal collectively with them on their own plane would have been preferable to that to which Quiggin had somehow steered us all.

" What was the flick like?" Templer enquired.

" Marvellous," said Mona. " The sweetest—no, really— but *the* sweetest little girl you ever saw."

" She was awfully good," said Jean.

" But what happened?"

" Well, this little girl—who was called Manuela—was sent to a very posh German school."

"*Posh?*" said Templer. "Sweetie, what an awful word. Please never use it in my presence again."

Rather to my surprise, Mona accepted this rebuke meekly: even blushing slightly.

"Well, Manuela went to this school, and fell *passionately* in love with one of the mistresses."

"What did I tell you?" said Templer. "Nick insisted the film wasn't about lesbians. You see he just poses as a man of the world, and hasn't really the smallest idea what is going on round him."

"It isn't a bit what *you* mean," said Mona, now bursting with indignation. "It was a really beautiful story. Manuela tried to *kill* herself. I cried and cried and cried."

"It really was good," said Jean to me. "Have you seen it?"

"Yes. I liked it."

"He's lying," said Templer. "If he had seen the film he would have known it was about lesbians. Look here, Nick, why not come home with us for the week-end? We can run you back to your flat and get a toothbrush. I should like you to see our house, uncomfortable as staying there will be."

"Yes, *do* come, darling," said Mona, drawing out the words with her absurd articulation. "You will find everything quite mad, I'm afraid."

She had by then drunk rather a lot of champagne.

"You must come," said Jean, speaking in her matter-of-fact tone, almost as if she were giving an order. "There are all sorts of things I want to talk about."

"Of course he'll come," said Templer. "But we might have the smallest spot of armagnac first."

Afterwards, that dinner in the Grill seemed to partake of the nature of a ritual feast, a rite from which the four of us emerged to take up new positions in the formal

dance with which human life is concerned. At the time, its charm seemed to reside in a difference from the usual run of things. Certainly the chief attraction of the projected visit would be absence of all previous plan. But, in a sense, nothing in life is planned—or everything is—because in the dance every step is ultimately the corollary of the step before; the consequence of being the kind of person one chances to be.

While we were at dinner heavy snow was descending outside. This downfall had ceased by the time my things were collected, though a few flakes were still blowing about in the clear winter air when we set out at last for the Templers' house. The wind had suddenly dropped. The night was very cold.

"Had to sell the Buick," Templer said. "I'm afraid you won't find much room at the back of this miserable vehicle."

Mona, now comatose after the wine at dinner, rolled herself up in a rug and took the seat in front. Almost immediately she went to sleep. Jean and I sat at the back of the car. We passed through Hammersmith, and the neighbourhood of Chiswick: then out on to the Great West Road. For a time I made desultory conversation. At last she scarcely answered, and I gave it up. Templer, smoking a cigar in the front, also seemed disinclined to talk now that he was at the wheel. We drove along at a good rate.

On either side of the highway, grotesque buildings, which in daytime resembled the temples of some shoddy, utterly unsympathetic Atlantis, now assumed the appearance of an Arctic city's frontier forts. Veiled in snow, these hideous monuments of a lost world bordered a broad river of black, foaming slush, across the surface of which the car skim-

med and jolted with a harsh crackling sound, as if the liquid beneath were scalding hot.

Although not always simultaneous in taking effect, nor necessarily at all equal in voltage, the process of love is rarely unilateral. When the moment comes, a secret attachment is often returned with interest. Some know this by instinct; others learn in a hard school.

The exact spot must have been a few hundred yards beyond the point where the electrically illuminated young lady in a bathing dress dives eternally through the petrol-tainted air; night and day, winter and summer, never reaching the water of the pool to which she endlessly glides. Like some image of arrested development, she returns for ever, voluntarily, to the springboard from which she started her leap. A few seconds after I had seen this bathing belle journeying, as usual, imperturbably through the frozen air, I took Jean in my arms.

Her response, so sudden and passionate, seemed surprising only a minute or two later. All at once everything was changed. Her body felt at the same time hard and yielding, giving a kind of glow as if live current issued from it. I used to wonder afterwards whether, in the last resort, of all the time we spent together, however ecstatic, those first moments on the Great West Road were not the best.

To what extent the sudden movement that brought us together was attributable to sentiment felt years before; to behaviour that was almost an obligation within the Templer orbit; or, finally, to some specific impetus of the car as it covered an unusually bad surface of road, was later impossible to determine with certainty. All I knew was that I had not thought it all out beforehand. This may seem extraordinary in the light of what had gone before;

but the behaviour of human beings is, undeniably, extraordinary. The incredible ease with which this evolution took place was almost as if the two of us had previously agreed to embrace at that particular point on the road. The timing had been impeccable.

We had bowled along much farther through the winter night, under cold, glittering stars, when Templer turned the car off the main road. Passing through byways lined with beech trees, we came at last to a narrow lane where snow still lay thick on the ground. At the end of this, the car entered a drive, virginally white. In the clear moonlight the grotesquely gabled house ahead of us, set among firs, seemed almost a replica of that mansion by the sea formerly inhabited by Templer's father. Although smaller in size, the likeness of general outline was uncanny. I almost expected to hear the crash of wintry waves beneath a neighbouring cliff. The trees about the garden were powdered with white. Now and then a muffled thud resounded as snow fell through the branches on to the thickly coated ground. Otherwise, all was deathly silent.

Templer drew up with a jerk in front of the door, the wheels churning up the snow. He climbed quickly from his seat, and went round to the back of the car, to unload from the boot some eatables and wine they had brought from London. At the same moment Mona came out of her sleep or coma. With the rug still wrapped round her, she jumped out of her side of the car, and ran across the Sisley landscape to the front door, which someone had opened from within. As she ran she gave a series of little shrieks of agony at the cold. Her footprints left deep marks on the face of the drive, where the snow lay soft and tender, like the clean, clean sheets of a measureless bed.

" Where shall I find you?"

" Next to you on the left."

" How soon?"

" Give it half an hour."

" I'll be there."

" Don't be too long."

She laughed softly when she said that, disengaging herself from the rug that covered both of us.

The interior of the house was equally reminiscent of the Templers' former home. Isbister's huge portrait of Mr. Templer still hung in the hall, a reminder of everyday life and unsolved business problems. Such things seemed far removed from this mysterious, snowy world of unreality, where all miracles could occur. There were the same golf clubs and shooting-sticks and tennis racquets; the same barometer, marking the weather on a revolving chart; the same post-box for letters; even the same panelling in light wood that made the place seem like the interior of a vast, extravagant cabinet for cigars.

" What we need," said Templer, " is a drink. And then I think we shall all be ready for bed."

For a second I wondered whether he were aware that something was afoot; but, when he turned to help Mona with the bottles and glasses, I felt sure from their faces that neither had given a thought to any such thing.

THREE

Early in the morning, snow was still drifting from a darkened sky across the diamond lattices of the window-panes; floating drearily down upon the white lawns and grey muddy paths of a garden flanked by pines and fir trees. Through these coniferous plantations, which arose above thick laurel bushes, appeared at no great distance glimpses of two or three other houses similar in style to the one in which I found myself; the same red brick and gables, the same walls covered with ivy or virginia creeper.

This was, no doubt, a settlement of prosperous business men; a reservation, like those created for indigenous inhabitants, or wild animal life, in some region invaded by alien elements: a kind of refuge for beings unfitted to battle with modern conditions, where they might live their own lives, undisturbed and unexploited by an aggressive outer world. In these confines the species might be saved from extinction. I felt miles away from everything, lying there in that bedroom: almost as if I were abroad. The weather was still exceedingly cold. I thought over a conversation I had once had with Barnby.

"Has any writer ever told the truth about women?" he had asked.

One of Barnby's affectations was that he had read little or nothing, although, as a matter of fact, he knew rather thoroughly a small curiously miscellaneous collection of books.

"Few in this country have tried."

" No one would believe it if they did."

" Possibly. Nor about men either, if it comes to that."

" I intend no cheap cynicism," Barnby said. " It is merely that in print the truth is not credible for those who have not thought deeply of the matter."

" That is true of almost everything."

" To some extent. But painting, for example—where women are concerned—is quite different from writing. In painting you can state everything there is to be said on the subject. In other words, the thing is treated purely æsthetically, almost scientifically. Writers always seem to defer to the wishes of the women themselves."

" So do painters. What about Reynolds or Boucher?"

" Of course, of course," said Barnby, whose capacity for disregarding points made against him would have supplied the foundation for a dazzling career at the Bar. " But in writing—perhaps, as you say, chiefly writing in this country—there is no equivalent, say, of Renoir's painting. Renoir did not think that all women's flesh was *literally* a material like pink satin. He used that colour and texture as a convention to express in a simple manner certain pictorial ideas of his own about women. In fact he did so in order to get on with the job in other aspects of his picture. I never find anything like that in a novel."

" You find plenty of women with flesh like that sitting in the Ritz."

" Maybe. And I can paint them. But can you write about them?"

" No real tradition of how women behave exists in English writing. In France there is at least a good rough and ready convention, perhaps not always correct—riddled with every form of romanticism—but at least a pattern to which a writer can work. A French novelist may conform with the convention, or depart from it. His readers know,

more or less, which he is doing. Here, every female character has to be treated empirically."

"Well, after all, so does every woman," said Barnby, another of whose dialectical habits was suddenly to switch round and argue against himself. "One of the troubles, I think, is that there are too many novelists like St. John Clarke."

"But novelists of the first rank have not always been attracted to women, physically."

"If of the first rank," said Barnby, "they may rise above it. If anything less, homosexual novelists are, I believe, largely responsible for some of the extraordinary ideas that get disseminated about women and their behaviour."

Barnby's sententious tone had already indicated to me that he was himself entangled in some new adventure. Those utterances, which Mr. Deacon used to call "Barnby's generalisations about women," were almost always a prelude to a story involving some woman individually. So it had turned out on that occasion.

"When you first make a hit with someone," he had continued, "you think everything is going all right with the girl, just because it is all right with you. But when you are more used to things, you are always on your guard—prepared for trouble of one sort or another."

"Who is it this time?"

"A young woman I met on a train."

"How promiscuous."

"She inspired a certain confidence."

"And things are going wrong?"

"On the contrary, going rather well. That is what makes me suspicious."

"Have you painted her?"

Barnby rummaged among the brushes, tubes of paint,

newspapers, envelopes and bottles that littered the table; coming at last to a large portfolio from which he took a pencil drawing. The picture was of a girl's head. She looked about twenty. The features, suggested rather than outlined, made her seem uncertain of herself, perhaps on the defensive. Her hair was untidy. There was an air of self-conscious rebellion. Something about the portrait struck me as familiar.

"What is her name?"

"I don't know."

"Why not?"

"She won't tell me."

"How very secretive."

"That's what I think."

"How often has she been here?"

"Two or three times."

I examined the drawing again.

"I've met her."

"Who is she?"

"I'm trying to remember."

"Have a good think," said Barnby, sighing. "I like to clear these matters up."

But for the moment I was unable to recall the girl's name. I had the impression our acquaintance had been slight, and was of a year or two earlier. There had been something absurd, or laughable, in the background of the occasion when we had met.

"It would be only polite to reveal her identity by now," Barnby said, returning the drawing to the portfolio and making a grimace.

"How did it start?"

"I was coming back from a week-end with the Manaschs'. She arrived in the compartment about an hour be-

fore we reached London. We began to talk about films. For some reason we got on to the French Revolution. She said she was on the side of the People."

" Dark eyes and reddish hair?"

" The latter unbrushed."

" Christian name, Anne?"

" There was certainly an 'A' on her handkerchief. That was a clue I forgot to tell you."

" Generally untidy?"

" Decidedly. As to baths, I shouldn't think she overdid them."

" I think I can place her."

" Don't keep me in suspense."

" Lady Anne Stepney."

" A friend of yours?"

" I sat next to her once at dinner years ago. She made the same remark about the French Revolution."

" Did she, indeed," said Barnby, perhaps a shade piqued at this apparently correct guess. " Did you follow up those liberal convictions at the time?"

" On the contrary. I doubt if she would even remember my name. Her sister married Charles Stringham, whom I've sometimes talked of. They are getting a divorce, so I saw in the paper."

" Oh, yes," said Barnby. " I read about it too. Stringham was the Great Industrialist's secretary at one moment, wasn't he? I met him with Baby and liked him. He has that very decorative mother, Mrs. Foxe, whom really I wouldn't——"

He became silent; then returned to the subject of the girl.

" Her parents are called Bridgnorth?"

" That's it."

" One starts these things," Barnby said, " and then the

question arises: how is one to continue them? Before
you know where you are, you are thoroughly entangled.
That is what we all have to remember."

" We do, indeed."

Lying in bed in the Templers' house, feeling more than
a little unwilling to rise into a chilly world, I thought of
these words of Barnby's. There could be no doubt that I
was now, as he had said, " thoroughly entangled."

Everyone came down late to breakfast that morning.
Mona was in a decidedly bad temper. Her irritation was
perhaps due to an inner awareness that a love affair was in
the air, the precise location of which she was unable to
identify; for I was fairly certain that neither of the
Templers guessed anything was " on " between Jean and
myself. They seemed, indeed, fully occupied by the discord
of their own relationship. As it happened, I found no
opportunity to be alone with Jean. She seemed almost
deliberately to arrange that we should always be chaperoned
by one of the other two. She would once more have
appeared as calm, distant, unknown to me, as when first
seen, had she not twice smiled submissively, almost shyly,
when our eyes met.

Mona's sulkiness cast a gloom over the house. Although
obviously lazy and easy-going in her manner of life, she
possessed also an energy and egotism that put considerable
force behind this display of moodiness. Templer made
more than one effort to cheer her up, from time to time
becoming annoyed himself at his lack of success; when
conciliation would suddenly turn to teasing. However, his
continued attempts to fall in with his wife's whims led in
due course to an unexpected development in the composition of the party.

We were sitting in a large room of nebulous character,
where most of the life of the household was carried on,

reading the Sunday papers, talking, and playing the gramophone. The previous night's encounter with Quiggin had enflamed Mona's memories of her career as an artist's model. She began to talk of the " times " she had had in various studios, and to question me about Mark Members; perhaps regretting that she had allowed this link with her past to be severed so entirely. Professionally, she had never come across such figures as Augustus John, or Epstein, trafficking chiefly with a group of the lesser academic painters; though she had known a few young men, like Members and Barnby, who frequented more " advanced " circles. She had never even sat for Isbister, so she told me. All the same, that period of her life was now sufficiently far away to be clouded with romance; at least when compared in her own mind with her married circumstances.

When I agreed that both Members and Quiggin were by then, in their different ways, quite well-known " young writers," she became more than ever enthusiastic about them, insisting that she must meet Quiggin again. In fact conversation seemed to have been deliberately steered by her into these channels with that end in view. Templer, lying in an armchair with his legs stretched out in front of him, listened indifferently to her talk while he idly turned the pages of the *News of the World*. His wife's experiences among " artists " probably cropped up fairly often as a subject : a regular, almost legitimate method of exciting a little domestic jealousy when life at home seemed flat. Her repeated questions at last caused me to explain the change of secretary made by St. John Clarke.

" But this is all *too* thrilling," she said. " I told you St. John Clarke was my favourite author. Can't we get Mr. Quiggin to lunch and ask him what really *has* happened?"

" Well——"

" Look, Pete," she exclaimed noisily. " *Do* let's ask J. G.

Quiggin to lunch to-day. He could get a train. Nick would ring him up—you will, won't you, darling?"

Templer threw the *News of the World* on to the carpet, and, turning towards me, raised his eyebrows and nodded his head slowly up and down to indicate the fantastic lengths to which caprice could be carried by a woman.

"But would Mr. Quiggin want to come?" he asked, imitating Mona's declamatory tone. "Wouldn't he want to finish writing one of his brilliant articles?"

"We could try."

"By all means, if you like. Half-past eleven on the day of the luncheon invitation is considered a bit late in the best circles, but fortunately we do not move in the best circles. I suppose there will be enough to eat. You remember Jimmy is bringing a girl friend?"

"Jimmy doesn't matter."

"I agree."

"What do you think, Nick?" she asked. "Would Quiggin come?"

One of the charms of staying with the Templers had seemed the promise of brief escape from that routine of the literary world so relentlessly implied by the mere thought of Quiggin. It was the world in which I was thoroughly at home, and certainly did not wish to change for another, only for once to enjoy a week-end away from it. However, to prevent the Templers from asking Quiggin to lunch if they so desired was scarcely justifiable to anyone concerned. Besides, I was myself curious to hear further details regarding St. John Clarke; although I should have preferred by then to have heard Members's side of the story. Apart from all that—indeed quite overriding such considerations—were my own violent feelings about Jean which had to be reduced inwardly to some manageable order.

" Who is ' Jimmy '?" I asked.

" Surely you remember Jimmy Stripling when you stayed with us years ago?" said Templer. " My brother-in-law. At least he was until Babs divorced him. Somehow I've never been able to get him out of my life. Babs can demand her freedom and go her own way. For me there is no legal redress. Jimmy hangs round my neck like a millstone. I can't even get an annulment."

" Didn't he go in for motor racing?"

" That's the chap."

" Who disliked Sunny Farebrother so much?"

" Hated his guts. Well, Jimmy is coming to lunch to-day and bringing some sort of a piece with him—he asked if he could. Not too young, I gather, so your eyes need not brighten up. I can't remember her name. I could not refuse for old times' sake, though he is a terrible bore is poor old Jimmy these days. He had a spill at Brooklands a year or two ago. Being shot out of his car arse-first seems to have affected his brain in some way—though you wouldn't think there was much there to affect."

" What does he do?"

" An underwriter at Lloyd's. It is not his business capacity so much as his private life that has seized up. He still rakes in a certain amount of dough. But he has taken up astrology and theosophy and numerology and God knows what else. Could your friend Quiggin stand that? Probably love it, wouldn't he? The more the merrier so far as I'm concerned."

" Quiggin would eat it up."

" *Do* ring him, then," said Mona.

" Shall I?"

" Go ahead," said Templer. " The telephone is next door."

There was no reply from Quiggin's Bloomsbury flat, so I rang St. John Clarke's number; on the principle that if a thing is worth doing, it is worth doing well. The bell buzzed for some seconds, and then Quiggin's voice sounded gratingly at the other end of the line. As I had supposed, he was already engaged on his new duties. At first he was very suspicious of my seeking him out at that place. These suspicions were not allayed when I explained about the invitation to lunch with the Templers.

"But *to-day*?" he said, irritably. "Lunch to-day? Why, it's nearly lunch-time already."

I repeated to him Mona's apologies for the undoubted lateness of the invitation.

"But I don't know them," said Quiggin. "Are they very rich?"

He still sounded cross, although a certain interest was aroused in him. I referred again to his earlier meeting with Mona.

"So she remembered me at Deacon's party after all?" he asked, rather more hopefully this time.

"She has talked of nothing but that evening."

"I don't think I ought to leave St. J."

"Is he bad?"

"Better, as a matter of fact. But there ought to be some-one responsible here."

"Couldn't you get Mark?" I asked, to tease him.

"St. J. does not want to see Mark just at the moment," said Quiggin, in his flattest voice, ignoring any jocular implications the question might have possessed. "But I suppose there is really no reason why the maid should not look after him perfectly well if I went out for a few hours."

This sounded like weakening.

"You could catch the train if you started now."

He was silent for a moment, evidently anxious to accept, but at the same time trying to find some excuse for making himself so easily available.

" Mona reads your articles."

" She does?"

" Always quoting them."

" Intelligently?"

" Come and judge for yourself."

" Should I like their house?"

" You'll have the time of your life."

" I think I will," he said. " Of course I shall be met at the station?"

" Of course."

" All right, then."

He replaced the receiver with a bang, as if closing an acrimonious interchange. I returned to the drawing-room. Templer was sprawling on the sofa, apparently not much interested whether Quiggin turned up or not.

" He's coming."

" Is he *really*?" said Mona, shrilly. " How *wonderful*."

" Mona gets a bit bored with my friends," said Templer. " I must say I don't blame her. Now you can sample something of another kind at lunch, sweetie."

" Well, we never see anybody *interesting*, sweetie," said Mona, putting on a stage pout. " He'll at least remind me of the days when I *used* to meet intelligent people."

" Intelligent people?" said Templer. " Come, come, darling, you aren't being very polite to Nick. He regards himself as tremendously intelligent."

" Then we are providing some intelligent company for him," said Mona. " Your ex-brother-in-law isn't likely to come out with anything very sparkling in the way of conversation—unless he has changed a lot since we went with him to Wimbledon."

"What do you expect at Wimbledon?" said Templer. "To sit in the centre court listening to a flow of epigrams about foot-faults and forehand drives? Still, I see what you mean."

I remembered Jimmy Stripling chiefly on account of various practical jokes in which he had been concerned when, as a boy, I had stayed with the Templers. In this horseplay he had usually had the worst of it. He remained in my memory as a big, gruff, bad-tempered fellow, full of guilty feelings about having taken no part in the war. I had not much cared for him. I wondered how he would get on with Quiggin, who could be crushing to people he disliked. However, one of the traits possessed by Quiggin in common with his new employer was a willingness to go almost anywhere where a free meal was on offer; and this realistic approach to social life implied, inevitably, if not toleration of other people, at least a certain rough and ready technique for dealing with all sorts. I could not imagine why Mona was so anxious to see Quiggin again. At that time I failed entirely to grasp the extent to which in her eyes Quiggin represented high romance.

"What happened to Babs when she parted from Jimmy Stripling?"

"Married a lord," said Templer. "The family is going up in the world. But I expect she still thinks about Jimmy. After all, you couldn't easily forget a man with breath like his."

Some interruption changed the subject before I was able to ask the name of Babs's third husband. Mona went to tell the servants that there would be an additional guest. Templer followed her to look for more cigarettes. For a moment Jean and I were left alone together. I slipped my hand under her arm. She pressed down upon it, giving me a sense of being infinitely near to her; an assurance that

all would be well. There is always a real and an imaginary person you are in love with; sometimes you love one best, sometimes the other. At that moment it was the real one I loved. We had scarcely time to separate and begin a formal conversation when Mona returned to the room.

There the four of us remained until the sound came of a car churning up snow before the front door. This was Quiggin's arrival. Being, in a way, so largely responsible for his presence at the Templers' house, I was relieved to observe, when he entered the room, that he had cleaned himself up a bit since the previous evening. Now he was wearing a suit of cruelly blue cloth and a green knitted tie. From the start it was evident that he intended to make himself agreeable. His sharp little eyes darted round the walls, taking in the character of his hosts, and their house.

"I see you have an Isbister in the hall," he said, dryly.

The harsh inflexion of his voice made it possible to accept this comment as a compliment, or, alternatively, a shared joke. Templer at once took the words in the latter sense.

"Couldn't get rid of it," he said. "I suppose you don't know anybody who would make an offer? An upset price, of course. Now's the moment."

"I'll look about," said Quiggin. "Isbister was a typical artist-business man produced by a decaying society, don't you think? As a matter of fact Nicholas and I have got to have a talk about Isbister in the near future."

He grinned at me. I hoped he was not going to raise the whole question of St. John Clarke's introduction there and then. His tone might have meant anything or nothing, so far as his offer of help was concerned. Perhaps he really intended to suggest that he would try to sell the picture for Templer, and get a rake-off. His eyes continued to stray

over the very indifferent nineteenth-century seascapes that covered the walls; hung together in patches as if put up hurriedly when the place was first occupied. No doubt that was exactly what had happened to them. In the Templers' house by the sea they had hung in the dining-room. Before the Isbister could be discussed further, the two other guests arrived.

The first through the door was a tall, rather overpowering lady, followed closely by Jimmy Stripling himself, looking much older than I had remembered him. The smoothness of the woman's movements, as she advanced towards Mona, almost suggested that Stripling was propelling her in front of him like an automaton on castors. I knew at once that I had seen her before, but could not at first recall the occasion : one so different, as it turned out, from that of the moment.

" How are you, Jimmy?" said Templer.

Stripling took the woman by the arm.

" This is Mrs. Erdleigh," he said, in a strangled voice. " I have told you so much about her, you know, and here she is."

Mrs. Erdleigh shook hands graciously all round, much as if she were a visiting royalty. When she came to me, she took my hand in hers and smiled indulgently.

" You see I was right," she said. " You did not believe me, did you? It is just a year."

Once more, suffocating waves of musk-like scent were distilled by her presence. By then, as a matter of fact, a month or two must have passed beyond the year that she had foretold would precede our next meeting. All the same, it was a respectable piece of prognostication. I thought it wiser to leave Uncle Giles unmentioned. If she wished to speak of him, she could always raise the subject

herself. I reflected, at the same time, how often this exterior aspect of Uncle Giles's personality must have remained "unmentioned" throughout his life; especially where his relations were concerned.

However, Mrs. Erdleigh gave the impression of knowing very well what was advisable to "mention" and what inadvisable. She looked well; younger, if anything, than when I had seen her at the Ufford, and smartly dressed in a style that suggested less than before her inexorably apocalyptic role in life. In fact, her clothes of that former occasion seemed now, in contrast, garments of a semi-professional kind; vestments, as it were, appropriate to the ritual of her vocation. With Stripling under her control—as he certainly was—she could no doubt allow herself frivolously to enjoy the fashion of the moment.

Stripling himself, on the other hand, had changed noticeably for the worse in the ten years or more gone since our former meeting. His bulk still gave the impression that he was taking up more than his fair share of the room, but the body, although big, seemed at the same time shrivelled. His hair, still parted in the middle, was grey and grizzled. Although at that time still perhaps under forty, he looked prematurely old. There was an odd, disconnected stare in his eyes, which started from his head when he spoke at all emphatically. He appeared to be thoroughly under the thumb of Mrs. Erdleigh, whose manner, kindly though firm, implied supervision of a person not wholly responsible for his own actions. Later, it was noticeable how fixedly he watched her, while in conversation he inclined to refer even the most minor matters to her arbitration. In spite of his cowed air, he was far more friendly than when we had met before, an occasion he assured me he remembered perfectly.

"We had a lot of fun that summer with my old pal,

Sunny Farebrother, didn't we?" he said in a melancholy voice.

He spoke as if appealing for agreement that the days when fun could be had with Sunny Farebrother, or indeed with anyone else, were now long past.

" Do you remember how we were going to put a po in his hat-box or something?" he went on. " How we all laughed. Good old Sunny. I never seem to see the old boy now, though I hear he's making quite a bit of money. It's just the same with so many folks one used to know. They pass by on the other side or join the Great Majority."

His face had lighted up when, upon entering the room, he had seen Jean, and he had taken both her hands in his and kissed her enthusiastically. She did not seem to regard this act as anything out of the way, nor even specially repugnant to her. I felt a twinge of annoyance at that kiss. I should have liked no one else to kiss her for at least twenty-four hours. However, I reminded myself that such familiarity was reasonable enough in an ex-brother-in-law; in fact, if it came to that, reasonable enough in any old friend; though for that reason no more tolerable to myself. Stripling also held Jean's arm for a few seconds, but, perhaps aware of Mrs. Erdleigh's eye upon him, removed his hand abruptly. Fumbling in his pocket, he produced a long gold cigarette-case and began to fill it from a packet of Players. Although physically dilapidated, he still gave the impression of being rich. The fact that his tweeds were crumpled and the cuffs of his shirt greasy somehow added to this impression of wealth. If there had been any doubt about Stripling's money, his satisfactory financial position could have been estimated from Quiggin's manner towards him, a test like litmus paper where affluence was concerned. Quiggin was evidently anxious—as I was myself—to learn more of this strange couple.

"How's the world, Jimmy?" said Templer, clapping his former brother-in-law on the back, and catching my eye as he handed him an unusually stiff drink.

"Well," said Stripling, speaking slowly, as if Templer's enquiry deserved very serious consideration before an answer was made, "well, I don't think the *World* will get much better as long as it clings to material values."

At this Quiggin laughed in a more aggressive manner than he had adopted hitherto. He was evidently trying to decide whether it would be better to be ingratiating to Stripling or to attack him; either method could be advantageous from its respective point of view.

"*I* think material values are just what want reassessing," Quiggin said. "Nor do I see how we can avoid clinging to them, since they are the only values that truly exist. However, they might be linked with a little social justice for a change."

Stripling disregarded this remark, chiefly, I think, because his mind was engrossed with preoccupations so utterly different that he had not the slightest idea what Quiggin was talking about. Templer's eyes began to brighten as he realised that elements were present that promised an enjoyable clash of opinions. Luncheon was announced. We passed into the dining-room. As I sat down at the table I saw Mrs. Erdleigh's forefinger touch Mona's hand.

"As soon as I set eyes on you, my dear," she said, gently, "I knew that you belonged to the Solstice of Summer. When *is* your birthday?"

As usual, her misty gaze seemed to envelop completely whomsoever she addressed. There could be no doubt that her personality had immediately delighted Mona, who had by then already lost all her earlier sulkiness. Indeed, as the meal proceeded, Mrs. Erdleigh showed herself to be just what Mona had required. She provided limitlessly a

kind of conversational balm at once maternal and sacerdotal. The two of them settled down to a detailed discussion across the table of horoscopes and their true relation to peculiarities of character. I was for some reason reminded of Sillery dealing with some farouche undergraduate whom he wished especially to enclose within his net. Even Mona's so recently excited interest in Quiggin was forgotten in this torrent of astrological self-examination, systematically controlled, in spite of its urgency of expression by such a sympathetic informant. Mona seemed now entirely absorbed in Mrs. Erdleigh, whose manner, vigorous, calm, mystical, certainly dominated the luncheon table.

The meal passed off, therefore, with more success than might have been expected from such oddly assorted company. I reflected, not for the first time, how mistaken it is to suppose there exists some " ordinary " world into which it is possible at will to wander. All human beings, driven as they are at different speeds by the same Furies, are at close range equally extraordinary. This party's singular composition was undoubtedly enhanced by the commonplace nature of its surroundings. At the same time it was evident that the Templers themselves saw nothing in the least out-of-the-way about the guests collected round their table for Sunday luncheon; except possibly the fact that both Quiggin and I were professionally connected with books.

If Quiggin disapproved—and he did undoubtedly disapprove—of the turn taken by Mona's and Mrs. Erdleigh's talk, he made at first no effort to indicate his dissatisfaction. He was in possession of no clue to the fact that he had been arbitrarily deposed from the position of most honoured guest in the house that day. In any case, as a person who himself acted rarely if ever from frivolous or disinterested

motives, he would have found it hard, perhaps impossible, to understand the sheer irresponsibility of his invitation. To have been asked simply and solely on account of Mona's whim, if he believed that to be the reason, must have been in itself undeniably flattering to his vanity; but, as Mr. Deacon used sadly to remark, "those who enjoy the delights of caprice must also accustom themselves to bear caprice's lash." Even if Quiggin were aware of this harsh law's operation, he had no means of appreciating the ruthless manner in which it had been put into execution that afternoon. Mona's wish to see him had been emphasised by me when I had spoken with him on the telephone. If she continued to ignore him, Quiggin would logically assume that for one reason or another either Templer, or I myself, must have desired his presence. He would suspect some ulterior motive as soon as he began to feel sceptical as to Mona's interest in him being the cause of his invitation. As the meal progressed, this lack of attention on her part undoubtedly renewed earlier suspicions. By the time we were drinking coffee he was already showing signs of becoming less amenable.

I think this quite fortuitous situation brought about by the presence of Mrs. Erdleigh was not without effect on Quiggin's future behaviour towards Mona herself. If Mrs. Erdleigh had not been at the table he would undoubtedly have received the full force of his hostess's admiration. This would naturally have flattered him, but his shrewdness would probably also have assessed her deference as something fairly superficial. As matters turned out, apparent disregard for him keenly renewed his own former interest in her. Perhaps Quiggin thought she was deliberately hiding her true feelings at luncheon. Perhaps he was right in thinking that With a woman it is impossible to say.

In the early stages of the meal Quiggin had been per-

fectly agreeable, talking to Jean of changes taking place in contemporary poetry, and of the personalities involved in these much advertised literary experiments. He explained that he considered the work of Mark Members commendable, if more than a trifle old-fashioned.

" Mark has developed smoothly from beginnings legitimately influenced by Browning, paused perhaps too long in byways frequented by the Symbolists, and reached in his own good time a categorically individual style and phraseology. Unfortunately his *œuvre* is at present lacking in any real sense of social significance."

He glanced at Mona after saying this, perhaps hoping that a former friend of Gypsy Jones might notice the political implications of his words. However he failed to catch her attention, and turned almost immediately to lighter matters, evidently surprising even Templer by sagacious remarks regarding restaurant prices in the South of France, and an unexpected familiarity with the *Barrio chino* quarter in Barcelona. However, in spite of this conversational versatility, I was aware that Quiggin was inwardly turning sour. This could be seen from time to time in his face, especially in the glances of dislike he was beginning to cast in the direction of Stripling. He had probably decided that, rich though Stripling might be, he was not worth cultivating.

Stripling, for his part, did not talk much; when he spoke chiefly addressing himself to Jean. He had shown—perhaps not surprisingly—no interest whatever in Quiggin's admirably lucid exposition of the New School's poetic diction, in which Communist convictions were expressed in unexpected metre and rhyme. On the other hand Stripling did sometimes rouse himself in an attempt to break into the stream of astrological chatter that bubbled between Mrs. Erdleigh and Mona. His mind seemed to wander

perpetually through the mystic territories of clairvoyance, a world of the spirit no doubt incarnate to him in Mrs. Erdleigh herself. Although this appearance of permanent preoccupation, coupled with his peculiar, jerky manner, conveyed the impression that he might not be quite sane, Templer seemed to attach more importance to Stripling's City gossip than his father had ever done. Mr. Templer, I remembered, had been very curt with his son-in-law when financial matters were in question.

All the while I felt horribly bored with the whole lot of them, longing to be alone once more with Jean, and yet also in some odd manner almost dreading the moment when that time should come; one of those mixed sensations so characteristic of intense emotional excitement. There is always an element of unreality, perhaps even of slight absurdity, about someone you love. It seemed to me that she was sitting in an awkward, almost melodramatic manner, half-turned towards Quiggin, while she crumbled her bread with fingers long and subtly shaped. I seemed to be looking at a picture of her, yet felt that I could easily lose control of my senses, and take her, then and there, in my arms.

"But in these days you can't believe in such things as astrology," said Quiggin. "Why, even apart from other considerations, the very astronomical discoveries made since the time of the ancients have negatived what was once thought about the stars."

We had returned to the drawing-room. Already it was obvious that the afternoon must be spent indoors. The leaden, sunless sky, from which sleet was now falling with a clatter on to the frozen snow of the lawn, created in the house an atmosphere at once gloomy and sinister: a climate in itself hinting of necromancy. The electric light had to be turned on, just as if we were sitting in the lounge of the

Ufford. The heavy claret drunk at luncheon prompted a desire to lie at full length on the sofa, or at least to sit well back and stretch out the legs and yawn. For a second —soft and exciting and withdrawn immediately—I felt Jean's hand next to mine on the cushion. Quiggin lurked in the corners of the room, pretending to continue his examination of the pictures, his silence scarcely concealing the restlessness that had overtaken him. From time to time he shot out a remark, more or less barbed. He must by then have tumbled to the implications of his own status at the party. Nettled at Mrs. Erdleigh's capture of Mona, he was probably planning how best to express his irritation openly.

" Oh but I *do*," said Mona, drawling out the words. " I think those occult things are almost always right. They are in my case, I *know*."

" Yes, yes," said Quiggin, brushing aside this affirmation with a tolerant grin, as the mere fancy of a pretty girl, and at the same time addressing himself more directly to Stripling, at whom his first attack had certainly been aimed, " but *you* can't believe all that—a hard-headed business man like yourself?"

" That's just it," said Stripling, ignoring, in fact probably not noticing, the sneering, disagreeable tone of Quiggin's voice. " It's just the fact that I *am* occupied all day long with material things that makes me realise they are not the whole of life."

However, his eyes began to start from his head, so that he was perhaps becoming aware that Quiggin was deliberately teasing him. No doubt he was used to encountering a certain amount of dissent from his views, though opposition was probably not voiced as usual in so direct and dialectical a manner as this. Quiggin continued to smile derisively.

" You certainly find in me no champion of the City's methods," he said. " But at least what you call ' material things ' represent reality."

" Hardly at all."

" Oh, come."

" Money is a delusion."

" Not if you haven't got any."

" That is just when you realise most money's unreality."

" Why not get rid of yours, then?"

" I might any day."

" Let me know when you decide to."

" You must understand the thread that runs through life," said Stripling, now speaking rather wildly, and looking stranger than ever. " It does not matter that there may be impurities and errors in one man's method of seeking the Way. What matters is that he *is* seeking it—and knows there is a Way to be found."

" Commencement—Opposition—Equilibrium," said Mrs. Erdleigh in her softest voice, as if to offer Stripling some well-earned moral support. " You can't get away from it— Thesis—Antithesis—Synthesis."

" That's just what I mean," said Stripling, as if her words brought him instant relief. " Brahma—Vishnu— Siva."

" It all sounded quite Hegelian until you brought in the Indian gods," said Quiggin angrily.

He would no doubt have continued to argue had not a new element been introduced at this moment by Jean: an object that became immediately the focus of attention.

While this discussion had been in progress she had slipped from the room. I had been wondering how I could myself quietly escape from the others and look for her, when she returned carrying in her hand what first appeared to be a small wooden palette for oil paints. Two castors,

or wheels, were attached to this heart-shaped board, the far end of which was transfixed with a lead pencil. I recalled the occasion when Sunny Farebrother had ruined so many of Stripling's starched collars in a patent device in which he had a business interest, and I wondered whether this was something of a similar kind. However, Mrs. Erdleigh immediately recognised the significance of the toy and began to laugh a little reprovingly.

" Planchette?" she said. " You know, I really rather disapprove. I do not think Good Influences make themselves known through Planchette as a rule. And the things it writes cause such a lot of bad feeling sometimes."

" It really belongs to Baby," said Jean. " She heard of it somewhere and made Sir Magnus Donners get her one. She brought it round to us once when she was feeling depressed about some young man of hers. We couldn't make it work. She forgot to take it away and I have been carrying it round—meaning to give it back to her—ever since."

Stripling's eyes lit up and began once more to dilate.

" Shall we do it?" he asked, in a voice that shook slightly. " Do let's."

" Well," said Mrs. Erdleigh, speaking kindly, as if to a child who has proposed a game inevitably associated with the breakage of china, " I *know* trouble will come of it if we do."

" But for once," begged Stripling. " Don't you think for once, Myra? It's such a rotten afternoon."

" Then don't complain afterwards that I did not warn you."

Although I had often heard of Planchette, I had never, as it happened, seen the board in operation; and I felt some curiosity myself to discover whether its writings would indeed set down some of the surprising disclosures occasionally described by persons in the habit of playing

with it. The very name was new to both the Templers. Stripling explained that the machine was placed above a piece of blank paper, upon which the pencil wrote words, when two or three persons lightly rested their fingers upon the wooden surface: castors and pencil point moving without deliberate agency. Stripling was obviously delighted to be allowed for once to indulge in this forbidden practice, in spite of Mrs. Erdleigh's tempered disparagement. Whether her disapproval was really deep-seated, or due merely to a conviction that the game was unwise in that particular company, could only be guessed.

Quiggin was plainly annoyed; even rather insulted, at this step taken towards an actual physical attempt to invoke occult forces.

" I thought such things had been forgotten since the court of Napoleon III," he said. " You don't really believe it will write anything, do you?"

" You may be surprised by the knowledge it displays of your own life, old chap," said Stripling, with an effort to recover the breeziness of earlier days.

" Obviously—when someone is rigging it."

" It's hardly possible to rig it, old chap. You try and write something, just using the board by yourself. You'll find it damned difficult."

Quiggin gave an annoyed laugh. Some sheets of foolscap, blue and ruled with red lines for keeping accounts, were found in a drawer. One of these large sheets of paper was set out upon a table. The experiment began with Mona, Stripling and Mrs. Erdleigh as executants, the last of whom, having once registered her protest, showed no ungraciousness in her manner of joining the proceedings, if they were fated to take place. Templer obviously felt complete scepticism regarding the whole matter, which he could not be induced to take seriously even to the extent

of agreeing to participate. Quiggin, too, refused to join in, though he snowed an almost feverish interest in what was going forward.

Naturally, Quiggin was delighted when, after a trial of several minutes, no results whatever were achieved. Then the rest of us, in various combinations of persons, attempted to work the board. All these efforts were unsuccessful. Sometimes the pencil shot violently across the surface of the paper, covering sheet after sheet, as a new surface was substituted, with dashes and scribbles. More often, it would not move at all.

" You none of you seem to be getting very far," said Templer.

" It may be waste of time," said Mrs. Erdleigh. " Planchette can be very capricious. Perhaps there is an unsympathetic presence in the room."

" I should not be at all surprised," said Quiggin, speaking with elaborately satirical emphasis.

He stood with his heels on the fender, his hands in his pockets—rather in the position Le Bas used to adopt when giving a lecture on wiping your boots before coming into the house—very well pleased with the course things were taking.

" I think you are horrid," said Mona.

She made a face at him; in itself a sign of a certain renewed interest.

" I don't think you ought to believe in such things," said Quiggin, nasally.

" But I *do*."

She smiled encouragingly. She had probably begun to feel that occult phenomena, at least by its absence, was proving itself a bore; and that perhaps she might find more fun in returning to her original project of exploring Quiggin's own possibilities. However, this exchange be-

tween them was immediately followed by sudden development among the group resting their fingers on the board. Jean and Mona had been trying their luck with Stripling as third partner. Jean now rose from the table, and, dropping one of those glances at once affectionate and enquiring that raised such a storm within me, she said : " You have a go."

I took the chair and placed my fingers lightly where hers had been. Previously, when I had formed a trio with Mrs. Erdleigh and Mona—who had insisted on being party to every session— nothing of note had happened. Now, almost at once, Planchette began to move in a slow, regular motion.

At first, from the " feel " of the movement, I thought Stripling must be manipulating the board deliberately. A glassy look had come into his eye and his loose, rather brutal mouth sagged open. Then the regular, up-and-down rhythm came abruptly to an end. The pencil, as if impatient of all of us, shot off the paper on to the polished wood of the table. A sentence had been written. It was inverted from where Stripling was sitting. In fact the only person who could reasonably be accused of having written the words was myself. The script was long and sloping, Victorian in character. Mrs. Erdleigh took a step forward and read it aloud :

" *Karl is not pleased.*"

There was great excitement at this. Everyone crowded round our chairs.

" You must ask who 'Karl' is," said Mrs. Erdleigh, smiling.

She was the only one who remained quite unmoved by this sudden manifestation. Such things no longer surprised her. Quiggin, on the other hand, moved quickly round to my side of the table. He seemed divided between

a wish to accuse me of having written these words as a hoax, and at the same time an unwillingness to make the admission, obviously necessary in the circumstances, that any such deception must have required quite exceptional manipulative agility. In the end he said nothing, but stood there frowning hard at me.

"Is it Karl speaking?" asked Stripling, in a respectful, indeed reverential voice.

We replaced our hands on the board.

"*Who else*," wrote Planchette.

"Shall we continue?"

"*Antwortet er immer.*"

"Is that German?" said Stripling.

"What does it mean, Pete?" Mona called out shrilly.

Templer looked a little surprised at this.

"Isn't it: 'He always answers'?" he said. "My German is strictly commercial—not intended for communication with the Next World."

"Have you a message? Please write in English if you do not mind."

Stripling's voice again trembled a little when he said this.

"*Nothing to the Left.*"

This was decidedly enigmatic.

"Does he mean we should move the coffee tray?" Mona almost shouted, now thoroughly excited. "He doesn't say whose left. Perhaps we should clear the whole table."

Quiggin took a step nearer.

"Which of you is faking this?" he said roughly. "I believe it is you, Nick."

He was grinning hard, but I could see that he was extremely irritated. I pointed out that I could not claim to write neat Victorian calligraphy sideways, and also upside-down, at considerable speed: especially when unable to see the paper written upon.

"You must know ' Nothing to the Left ' is a quotation," Quiggin insisted.

"Who said it?"

"You got a degree in history, didn't you?"

"I must have missed out that bit."

"Robespierre, of course," said Quiggin, with great contempt. "He was speaking politically. Does no one in this country take politics seriously?"

I could not understand why he had become quite so angry.

"Let's get on with it," said Templer, now at last beginning to show some interest. "Perhaps he'll make himself clearer if pressed."

"This is *too* exciting," said Mona.

She clasped her hands together. We tried again.

"*Wives in common.*"

This was an uncomfortable remark. It was impossible to guess what the instrument might write next. However, everyone was far too engrossed to notice whether the comment had brought embarrassment to any individual present.

"Look here——" began Quiggin.

Before he could complete the sentence, the board began once more to race beneath our fingers.

"*Force is the midwife.*"

"I hope he isn't going to get too obstetric," said Templer.

Quiggin turned once more towards me. He was definitely in a rage.

"You must know where these phrases come from," he said. "You can't be as ignorant as that."

"Search me."

"You are trying to be funny."

"Never less."

"Marx, of course, Marx," said Quiggin testily, but perhaps wavering in his belief that I was responsible for faking the writing. "*Das Kapital.* . . . The Communist Manifesto."

"So it's Karl Marx, is it?" asked Mona.

The name was evidently vaguely familiar to her, no doubt from her earlier days when she had known Gypsy Jones; had perhaps even taken part in such activities as selling *War Never Pays!*

"Don't be ridiculous," said Quiggin, by implication including Mona in this reproof, probably more violently than he intended. "It was quite obvious that one of you was rigging the thing. I admit I can't at present tell which of you it was. I suspect it was Nick, as he is the only one who knows I am a practising Marxist—and he persuaded me to come here."

"I didn't know anything of the sort—and I've already told you I can't write upside-down."

"Steady on," said Templer. "You can't accuse a fellow guest of cheating at Planchette. Duels have been fought for less. This will turn into another Tranby Croft case unless we moderate our tone."

Quiggin made a despairing gesture at such frivolity of manner.

"I can't believe no one present knows the quotation, ' Force is the midwife of every old society pregnant with a new one,' " he said. "You will be telling me next you never heard the words, ' The Workers have no country.' "

"I believe Karl Marx has been ' through ' before," said Stripling, slowly and with great solemnity. "Wasn't he a revolutionary writer."

"He was," said Quiggin, with heavy irony. "He *was* a revolutionary writer."

" *Do* let's try again," said Mona.

This time the writing changed to a small, niggling hand, rather like that of Uncle Giles.

" *He is sick.*"

" Who is sick?"

" *You know well.*"

" Where is he?"

" *In his room.*"

" Where is his room?"

" *The House of Books.*"

The writing was getting smaller and smaller. I felt as if I were taking part in one of those scenes from *Alice in Wonderland* in which the characters change their size.

" What can it mean now?" asked Mona.

" *You have a duty.*"

Quiggin's temper seemed to have moved from annoyance, mixed with contempt, to a kind of general uneasiness.

" I suppose it isn't talking about St. John Clarke," I suggested.

Quiggin's reaction to this remark was unexpectedly violent. His sallow skin went white, and, instead of speaking with his usual asperity, he said in a quiet, worried voice : " I was beginning to wonder just the same thing. I don't know that I really ought to have left him. Look here, can I ring up the flat—just to make sure that everything is all right?"

" Of course," said Templer.

" This way?"

We tried again. Before Quiggin had reached the door, the board had moved and stopped. This time the result was disappointing. Planchette had written a single word, monosyllabic and indecent. Mona blushed.

" That sometimes happens," said Mrs. Erdleigh, calmly. She spoke as if it were as commonplace to see such things

written on blue ruled accounting paper as on the door or wall of an alley. Neatly detaching that half of the sheet, she tore it into small pieces and threw them into the waste-paper basket.

"Only too often," said Stripling with a sigh.

He had evidently accepted the fact that his enjoyment for that afternoon was at an end. Mona giggled.

"We will stop now," said Mrs. Erdleigh, speaking with the voice of authority. "It is really no use continuing when a Bad Influence once breaks through."

"I'm surprised he knew such a word," said Templer.

We sat for a time in silence. Quiggin's action in going to the telephone possessed the force of one of those utterly unexpected conversions, upon which a notorious drunkard swears never again to touch alcohol, or a declared pacifist enlists in the army. It was scarcely credible that Planchette should have sent him bustling out of the room to enquire after St. John Clarke's health, even allowing for the importance to himself of the novelist as a livelihood.

"We shall have to be departing soon, *mon cher*," said Mrs. Erdleigh, showing Stripling the face of her watch.

"Have some tea," said Templer. "It will be appearing at any moment."

"No, we shall certainly have to be getting along, Pete," said Stripling, as if conscious that, having been indulged over Planchette, he must now behave himself specially well. "It has been a wonderful afternoon. Quite like the old days. Wish old Sunny could have been here. Most interesting too."

He had evidently not taken in Quiggin's reason for hurrying to the telephone, nor had any idea of the surprising effect that Planchette's last few sentences had had on such a professional sceptic. Perhaps he would have been pleased to know that Quiggin had acquired at least enough

belief to be thrown into a nervous state by those cryptic
remarks. More probably, he would not have been greatly
interested. For Stripling, this had been a perfectly normal
manner of passing his spare time. He would never be able
to conceive how far removed were such activities from
Quiggin's daily life and manner of approaching the world.
In Stripling, profound belief had taken the place of any
sort of halting imagination he might once have claimed.

Quiggin now reappeared. He was even more disturbed
than before.

"I am afraid I must go home immediately," he said, in
some agitation. "Do you know when there is a train?
And can I be taken to the station? It is really rather
urgent."

"Is he dying?" asked Mona, in an agonised voice.

She was breathless with excitement at the apparent con-
firmation of a message from what Mrs. Erdleigh called
"the Other Side." She took Quiggin's arm, as if to soothe
him. He did not answer at once, apparently undecided at
what should be made public. Then he addressed himself
to me.

"The telephone was answered by Mark," he said,
through his teeth.

For Quiggin to discover Members reinstated in St. John
Clarke's flat within a few hours of his own departure was
naturally a serious matter.

"And *is* St. John Clarke worse?"

"I couldn't find out for certain," said Quiggin, almost
wretchedly, "but I think he must be for Mark to be
allowed back. I suppose St. J. wanted something done in a
hurry, and told the maid to ring up Mark as I wasn't there.
I must go at once."

He turned towards the Templers.

"I am afraid there is no train for an hour," Templer

said, "but Jimmy is on his way to London, aren't you, Jimmy? He will give you a lift."

"Of course, old chap, of course."

"Of course he can. So you can go with dear old Jimmy and arrive in London in no time. He drives like hell."

"No longer," said Mrs. Erdleigh, with a smile. "He drives with care."

I am sure that the last thing Quiggin wanted at that moment was to be handed over to Stripling and Mrs. Erdleigh, but there was no alternative if he wanted to get to London with the least possible delay. A curious feature of the afternoon had been the manner in which all direct contact between himself and Mrs. Erdleigh had somehow been avoided. Each no doubt realised to the full that the other possessed nothing to offer: that any exchange of energy would have been waste of time.

In Quiggin's mind, the question of St. John Clarke's worsened state of health, as such, had now plainly given place to the more immediate threat of Members re-entering the novelist's household on a permanent footing. His fear that the two-developments might be simultaneous was, I feel sure, not necessarily based upon entirely cynical premises. In a weakened state, St. John Clarke might easily begin to regret his earlier suspension of Members as a secretary. Sick persons often vacillate. Quiggin's anxiety was understandable. No doubt he regarded himself, politically and morally, as a more suitable secretary than Members. It was, therefore, reasonable that he should wish to return as soon as possible to the field of operations.

Recognising at once that he must inevitably accompany the two of them, Quiggin accepted Stripling's offer of conveyance. He did this with a bad grace, but at the same time insistently, to show there must be no delay now the matter had been decided. This sudden disintegration of the

party was displeasing to Mona, who probably felt now that she had wasted her opportunity of having Quiggin in the house; just as on the previous day she had wasted her meeting with him in the Ritz. She seemed, at any rate, overwhelmed with vague, haunting regrets for the manner in which things had turned out; all that unreasoning bitterness and mortification to which women are so subject. For a time she begged them to stay, but it was no good.

" But *promise* you will ring up."

She took Quiggin's hand. He seemed surprised, perhaps even rather touched at the warmth with which she spoke. He replied with more feeling than was usual in his manner that he would certainly communicate with her.

" I will let you know how St. J. is."

" Oh, *do*."

" Without fail."

" Don't forget."

Mrs. Erdleigh, in her travelling clothes, had reverted to my first impression of her at the Ufford as priestess of some esoteric cult. Wrapped about with scarves, veils and stoles, she took my hand.

" Have you met *her* yet?" she enquired in a low voice.

" Yes."

" Just as I told you?"

" Yes."

Mrs. Erdleigh smiled to herself. They piled into the car, Quiggin glowering in the back, hatless, but with a fairly thick overcoat. Stripling drove off briskly, sending the crisp snow in a shower from the wheels. The car disappeared into the gloomy shadows of the conifers.

We returned to the drawing-room. Templer threw himself into an arm-chair.

" What a party," he said. " Poor old Jimmy really has landed something this time. I wouldn't be surprised if he

didn't have to marry that woman. She's like Rider Haggard's *She—She who must be obeyed*."

"I thought she was wonderful," said Mona.

"So does Jimmy," said Templer. "You know, I can see a look of Babs. Something in the way she carries herself."

I, too, had noticed an odd, remote resemblance in Mrs. Erdleigh to his elder sister. However, Mona disagreed strongly, and they began to argue.

"It was extraordinary all that stuff about Marx coming up," said Templer. "I suppose it was swilling about in old Quiggin's head and somehow got released."

"Of course, you can never believe anything you can't explain quite simply," said Mona.

"Why should I?" said Templer.

Tea merged into drinks. Mona's temper grew worse. I began to feel distinctly tired. Jean had brought out some work, and was sewing. Templer yawned in his chair. I wondered why he and his wife did not get on better. It was extraordinary that he seemed to please so many girls, and yet not her.

"It was a pretty stiff afternoon," he said.

"I enjoyed it," said Mona. "It was a change."

"It certainly was."

They began to discuss Planchette again; ending inevitably in argument. Mona stood up.

"Let's go out to-night."

"Where to?"

"We could dine at Skindles."

"We've done that exactly a thousand and twenty-seven times. I've counted."

"Then the Ace of Spades."

"You know how I feel about the Ace of Spades after what happened to me there."

"But I like it."

" Anyway, wouldn't it be nicer to eat in to-night? Unless Nick and Jean are mad to make a night of it."

I had no wish to go out to dinner; Jean was non-committal. The Templers continued to argue. Suddenly Mona burst into tears.

" You never want to do *anything* I want," she said. " If I can't go out I shall go to bed. They can send up something on a tray. As a matter of fact I haven't been feeling well all day."

She turned from him, and almost ran from the room.

" Oh, hell," said Templer. " I suppose I shall have to see about this. Help yourselves to another drink when you're ready."

He followed his wife through the door. Jean and I were alone. She gave me her hand, smiling, but resisting a closer embrace.

" To-night?"

" No."

" Why not?"

" Not a good idea."

" I see."

" Sorry."

" When?"

" Any time."

" Will you come to my flat?"

" Of course."

" When?"

" I've told you. Any time you like."

" Tuesday?"

" No, not Tuesday."

" Wednesday, then?"

" I can't manage Wednesday either."

" But you said any time."

"Any time but Tuesday or Wednesday."

I tried to remember what plans were already made, and which could be changed. Thursday was a tangle of engagements, hardly possible to rearrange at short notice without infinite difficulties arising. Matters must be settled quickly, because Templer might return to the room at any moment.

"Friday?"

She looked doubtful. I thought she was going to insist on Thursday. Perhaps the idea of doing so had crossed her mind. A measure of capriciousness is, after all, natural in women; perhaps fulfils some physiological need for both sexes. A woman who loves you likes to torment you from time to time; if not actually hurt you. If her first intention had been to make further difficulties, she abandoned the idea, but at the same time she did not speak. She seemed to have no sense of the urgency of making some arrangement quickly—so that we should not lose touch with each other, and be reduced to the delay of writing letters. I suffered some agitation. This conversation was failing entirely to express my own feelings. Perhaps it seemed equally unreal to her. If so, she was unwilling, perhaps unable, to alleviate the strain. Probably women enjoy such moments, which undoubtedly convey by intensity and uncertainty a heightened awareness of their power. In spite of apparent coldness of manner her eyes were full of tears. As if we had already decided upon some definite and injudicious arrangement, she suddenly changed her approach.

"You must be discreet," she said.

"All right."

"But really discreet."

"I promise."

"You will?"

" Yes."

While talking, we had somehow come close together in a manner that made practical discussion difficult. I felt tired, and rather angry, and very much in love with her; on the edge of one of those outbursts of irritation so easily excited by love.

" I'll come to your flat on Friday," she said abruptly.

FOUR

When, in early spring, pale sunlight was flickering behind the mist above Piccadilly, the Isbister Memorial Exhibition opened on the upper floor of one of the galleries there. I was attending the private view, partly for business reasons, partly from a certain weakness for bad pictures, especially bad portraits. Such a taste is hard to justify. Perhaps the inclination is no more than a morbid curiosity to see how far the painter will give himself away. Pictures, apart from their æsthetic interest, can achieve the mysterious fascination of those enigmatic scrawls on walls, the expression of Heaven knows what psychological urge on the part of the executant; for example, the for ever anonymous drawing of Widmerpool in the *cabinet* at La Grenadière.

In Isbister's work there was something of that inner madness. The deliberate naïveté with which he accepted his businessmen, ecclesiastics and mayors, depicted by him with all the crudeness of his accustomed application of paint to canvas, conveyed an oddly sinister effect. Perhaps it would be more accurate to say that Isbister set out to paint what he supposed to be the fashionable view of such people at any given moment. Thus, in his early days, a general, or the chairman of some big concern, would be represented in the respectively appropriate terms of Victorian romantic success; the former, hero of the battlefield : the latter, the industrious apprentice who has achieved his worthy ambition. But as military authority and commercial achievement became increasingly subject to political and

economic denigration, Isbister, keeping up with the times, introduced a certain amount of what he judged to be satirical comment. Emphasis would be laid on the general's red face and medals, or the industrialist's huge desk and cigar. There would be a suggestion that all was not well with such people about. Probably Isbister was right from a financial point of view to make this change, because certainly his sitters seemed to grow no fewer. Perhaps they too felt a compulsive need for representation in contemporary idiom, even though a tawdry one. It was a kind of insurance against the attacks of people like Quiggin: a form of public apology and penance. The result was certainly curious. Indeed, often, even when there hung near-by something far worthier of regard, I found myself stealing a glance at an Isbister, dominating by its aggressive treatment, the other pictures hanging alongside.

If things had turned out as they should, *The Art of Horace Isbister* would have been on sale at the table near the door, over which a young woman with a pointed nose and black fringe presided. As things were, it was doubtful whether that volume would ever appear. The first person I saw in the gallery was Sir Gavin Walpole-Wilson, who stood in the centre of the room, disregarding the pictures, but watching the crowd over the top of huge horn-rimmed spectacles, which he had pushed well forward on his nose. His shaggy homespun overcoat was swinging open, stuffed with long envelopes and periodicals which protruded from the pockets. He looked no older; perhaps a shade less sane. We had not met since the days when I used to dine with the Walpole-Wilsons for " débutante dances;" a period now infinitely remote. Rather to my surprise he appeared to recognise me immediately, though it was unlikely that he knew my name. I enquired after Eleanor.

" Spends all her time in the country now," said Sir

Gavin. "As you may remember, Eleanor was never really happy away from Hinton."

He spoke rather sadly. I knew he was confessing his own and his wife's defeat. His daughter had won the long conflict with her parents. I wondered if Eleanor still wore her hair in a bun at the back and trained dogs with a whistle. It was unlikely that she would have changed much.

"I expect she finds plenty to do," I offered.

"Her breeding keeps her quiet," said Sir Gavin.

He spoke almost with distaste. However, perceiving that I felt uncertain as to the precise meaning of this explanation of Eleanor's existing state, he added curtly:

"Labradors."

"Like Sultan?"

"After Sultan died she took to breeding them. And then she sees quite a lot of her friend, Norah Tolland."

By common consent we abandoned the subject of Eleanor. Taking my arm, he led me across the floor of the gallery, until we stood in front of a three-quarter-length picture of a grey-moustached man in the uniform of the diplomatic corps; looking, if the truth be known, not unlike Sir Gavin himself.

"Isn't it terrible?"

"Awful."

"It's Saltonstall," said Sir Gavin, his voice suggesting that some just retribution had taken place. "Saltonstall who always posed as *a Man of Taste*."

"Isbister has made him look more like a Christmas Tree of Taste."

"You see, my father-in-law's portrait is a different matter," said Sir Gavin, as if unable to withdraw his eyes from this likeness of his former colleague. "There is no parallel at all. My father-in-law was painted by Isbister, it is true. Isbister was what he liked. He possessed a large

collection of thoroughly bad pictures which we had some difficulty in disposing of at his death. He bought them simply and solely because he liked the subjects. He knew about shipping and finance—not about painting. But he did not pose as a Man of Taste. Far from it."

"Deacon's *Boyhood of Cyrus* in the hall at Eaton Square is from his collection, isn't it?"

I could not help mentioning this picture that had once meant so much to me; and to name the dead is always a kind of tribute to them: one I felt Mr. Deacon deserved.

"I believe so," said Sir Gavin. "It sounds his style. But Saltonstall, on the other hand, with his *vers de societé*, and all his talk about Foujita and Pruna and goodness knows who else—but when it comes to his own portrait, it's Isbister. Let's see how they have hung my father-in-law."

We passed on to Lord Aberavon's portrait, removed from its usual place in the dining-room at Hinton Hoo, now flanked by Sir Horrocks Rusby, K.C., and Cardinal Whelan. Lady Walpole-Wilson's father had been painted in peer's robes over the uniform of a deputy-lieutenant, different tones of scarlet contrasted against a crimson velvet curtain: a pictorial experiment that could not be considered successful. Through french windows behind Lord Aberavon stretched a broad landscape—possibly the vale of Glamorgan—in which something had also gone seriously wrong with the colour values. Even Isbister himself, in his own lifetime, must have been aware of deficiency.

I glanced at the cardinal next door, notable as the only picture I had ever heard Widmerpool spontaneously praise. Here, too, the reds had been handled with some savagery. Sir Gavin shook his head and moved on to examine two of Isbister's genre pictures. "Clergyman eating an apple" and "The Old Humorists." I found myself beside Clap-

ham, a director of the firm that published St. John Clarke's novels. He was talking to Smethyck, a museum official I had known slightly at the university.

"When is your book on Isbister appearing?" Clapham asked at once. "You announced it some time ago. This would have been the moment—with the St. John Clarke introduction."

Clapham had spoken accusingly, his voice implying the fretfulness of all publishers that one of their authors should betray them with a colleague, however lightly.

"I went to see St. John Clarke the other day," Clapham continued. "I was glad to find him making a good recovery after his illness. Found him reading one of the young Communist poets. We had an interesting talk."

"Does anybody read St. John Clarke himself now?" asked Smethyck, languidly.

Like many of his profession, Smethyck was rather proud of his looks, which he had been carefully re-examining in the dark, mirror-like surface of Sir Horrocks Rusby, framed for some unaccountable reason under glass. Clapham was up in arms at once at such superciliousness.

"Of course people read St. John Clarke," he said, snappishly. "Though perhaps not in your ultra-sophisticated circles, where everything ordinary people understand is sneered at."

"Personally, I don't hold any views about St. John Clarke," said Smethyck, without looking round. "I've never read any of them. All I wanted to know was whether people bought his books."

He continued to ponder the cut of his suit in this adventitious looking-glass, deciding at last that his hair needed smoothing down on one side.

"I don't mind admitting to you both," said Clapham,

moving a step or two closer and speaking rather thickly, "that when I finished *Fields of Amaranth* there were tears in my eyes."

Smethyck made no reply to this; nor could I myself think of a suitable rejoinder.

"That was some years ago," said Clapham.

This qualification left open the alternative of whether St. John Clarke still retained the power of exciting such strong feeling in a publisher, or whether Clapham himself had grown more capable of controlling his emotions.

"Why, there's Sillery," said Smethyck, who seemed thoroughly bored by the subject of St. John Clarke. "I believe he was to be painted by Isbister, if he had recovered. Let's go and talk to him."

We left Clapham, still muttering about the extent of St. John Clarke's sales, and the beauty and delicacy of his early style. I had not seen Sillery since Mrs. Andriadis's party, three or four years before, though I had heard by chance that he had recently returned from America, where he had held some temporary academical post, or been on a lecture tour. His white hair and dark, Nietzschean moustache remained unchanged, but his clothes looked older than ever. He was carrying an unrolled umbrella in one hand; in the other a large black homburg, thick in grease. He began to grin widely as soon as he saw us.

"Hullo, Sillers," said Smethyck, who had been one of Sillery's favourites among the undergraduates who constituted his *salon*. "I did not know you were interested in art."

"Not interested in art?" said Sillery, enjoying this accusation a great deal. "What an idea. Still, I am, as it happens, here for semi-professional reasons, as you might say. I expect you are too, Michael. There is some nonsense

about the College wanting a pitcher o' me ole mug. Can't think why they should need such a thing, but there it is. 'Course Isbister can't do it 'cos 'e's tucked 'is toes in now, but I thought I'd just come an' take a look at the sorta thing that's expected."

" And what do you think, Sillers?"

" Just as well he's passed away, perhaps," sniggered Sillery, suddenly abandoning his character-acting. " In any case I always think an artist is rather an embarrassment to his own work. But what Ninetyish things I am beginning to say. It must come from talking to so many Americans."

" But you can't want to be painted by anyone even remotely like Isbister," said Smethyck. " Surely you can get a painter who is a little more modern than that. What about this man Barnby, for example?"

" Ah, we are very conservative about art at the older universities," said Sillery, grinning delightedly. " Wouldn't say myself that I want an Isbister exactly, though I heard the Warden comparing him with Antonio Moro the other night. 'Fraid the Warden doesn't know much about the graphic arts, though. But then *I* don't want the wretched picture painted at all. What do members of the College want to look at my old phiz for, I should like to know?"

We assured him that his portrait would be welcomed by all at the university.

" I don't know about Brightman," said Sillery, showing his teeth for a second. " I don't at all know about Brightman. I don't think Brightman would want a picture of me. But what have you been doing with yourself, Nicholas? Writing more books, I expect. I am afraid I haven't read the first one yet. Do you ever see Charles Stringham now?"

" Not for ages."

" A pity about that divorce," said Sillery. " You young

men will get married. It is so often a mistake. I hear he is drinking just a tiny bit too much nowadays. It was a mistake to leave Donners-Brebner, too."

"I expect you've heard about J. G. Quiggin taking Mark Members's place with St. John Clarke?"

"Hilarious that, wasn't it?" agreed Sillery. "That sort of thing always happens when two clever boys come from the same place. They can't help competing. Poor Mark seems quite upset about it. Can't think why. After all, there are plenty of other glittering prizes for those with stout hearts and sharp swords, just as Lord Birkenhead remarked. I shall be seeing Quiggin this afternoon, as it happens—a little political affair—Quiggin lives a very *mouvementé* life these days, it seems."

Sillery chuckled to himself. There was evidently some secret he did not intend to reveal. In any case he had by then prolonged the conversation sufficiently for his own satisfaction.

"Saw you chatting to Gavin Walpole-Wilson," he said. "Ought to go and have a word with him myself about these continuous hostilities between Bolivia and Paraguay. Been going on too long. Want to get in touch with his sister about it. Get one of her organisations to work. Time for liberal-minded people to step in. Can't have them cutting each other's throats in this way. Got to be quick, or I shall be late for Quiggin."

He shambled off. Smethyck smiled at me and shook his head, at the same time indicating that he had seen enough for one afternoon.

I strolled on round the gallery. I had noted in the catalogue a picture called "The Countess of Ardglass with Faithful Girl" and, when I arrived before it, I found Lady Ardglass herself inspecting the portrait. She was leaning on the arm of one of the trim grey-haired men who had

accompanied her in the Ritz: or perhaps another example of their category, so like as to be indistinguishable. Isbister had painted her in an open shirt and riding breeches, standing beside the mare, her arm slipped through the reins: with much attention to the high polish of the brown boots.

"Pity Jumbo could never raise the money for it," Bijou Ardglass was saying. "Why don't you make an offer, Jack, and give it me for my birthday? You'd probably get it dirt cheap."

"I'm much too broke," said the grey-haired man.

"You always say that. If you'd given me the car you promised me I should at least have saved the nine shillings I've already spent on taxis this morning."

Jean never spoke of her husband, and I knew no details of the episode with Lady Ardglass that had finally separated them. At the same time, now that I saw Bijou, I could not help feeling that she and I were somehow connected by what had happened. I wondered what Duport had in common with me that linked us through Jean. Men who are close friends tend to like different female types; perhaps the contrary process also operated, and the fact that he had seemed so unsympathetic when we had met years before was due to some innate sense of rivalry. I was to see Jean that afternoon. She had borrowed a friend's flat for a week or so, while she looked about for somewhere more permanent to live. This had made things easier. Emotional crises always promote the urgent need for executive action, so that the times when we most hope to be free from the practical administration of life are always those when the need to cope with a concrete world is more than ever necessary.

Owing to domestic arrangements connected with getting a nurse for her child, she would not be at home until late in the afternoon. I wasted some time at the Isbister show,

before walking across the park to the place where she was living. I had expected to see Quiggin at the gallery, but Sillery's remarks indicated that he would not be there. The last time I had met him, soon after the Templer week-end, it had turned out that, in spite of the temporary reappearance of Members at St. John Clarke's sick bed, Quiggin was still firmly established in his new position. He now seemed scarcely aware that there had ever been a time when he had not acted as the novelist's secretary, referring to his employer's foibles with a weary though tolerant familiarity, as if he had done the job for years. He had quickly brushed aside enquiry regarding his journey to London with Mrs. Erdleigh and Jimmy Stripling.

" What a couple," he commented.

I had to admit they were extraordinary enough. Quiggin had resumed his account of St. John Clarke, his state of health and his eccentricities, the last of which were represented by his new secretary in a decidedly different light from that in which they had been displayed by Members. St. John Clarke's every action was now expressed in Marxist terms, as if some political circle had overnight turned the novelist into an entirely Left Wing animal. No doubt Quiggin judged it necessary to handle his new situation firmly on account of the widespread gossip regarding St. John Clarke's change of secretary; for in circles frequented by Members and Quiggin ceaseless argument had taken place as to which of them had " behaved badly."

Thinking it best from my firm's point of view to open diplomatic relations, as it were, with the new government, I had asked if there was any hope of our receiving the Isbister introduction in the near future. Quiggin's answer to this had been to make an affirmative gesture with his hands. I had seen Members employ the same movement, perhaps derived by both of them from St. John Clarke himself.

" That was exactly what I wanted to discuss when I came to the Ritz," Quiggin had said. " But you insisted on going out with your wealthy friends."

" You must admit that I arranged for you to meet my wealthy friends, as you call them, at the first opportunity—within twenty-four hours, as a matter of fact."

Quiggin smiled and inclined his head, as if assenting to my claim that some amends had been attempted.

" As I have tried to explain," he said, " St. J.'s views have changed a good deal lately. Indeed, he has entirely come round to my own opinion—that the present situation cannot last much longer. *We will not tolerate it.* All thinking men are agreed about that. St. J. *wants* to do the introduction when his health gets a bit better—and he has time to spare from his political interests—but he has decided to write the Isbister foreword from a Marxist point of view."

" You ougnt to have obtained some first-hand information for him when Marx came through on Planchette."

Quiggin frowned at this levity.

" What rot that was," he said. " I suppose Mark and his psychoanalyst friends would explain it by one of their dissertations on the subconscious. Perhaps in that particular respect they would be right. No doubt they would add a lot of irrelevant stuff about Surrealism. But to return to Isbister's pictures, I think they would not make a bad subject treated in that particular manner."

" You could preach a whole Marxist sermon on the portrait of Peter Templer's father alone."

" You could, indeed," said Quiggin, who seemed not absolutely sure that the matter in hand was being negotiated with sufficient seriousness. " But what a charming person Mrs. Templer is. She has changed a lot since her days as a model, or mannequin, or whatever she was. It is a great pity she never seems to see any intelligent people now. I

can't think how she can stand that stockbroker husband of hers. How rich is he?"

" He took a bit of a knock in the slump."

" How do they get on together?"

" All right, so far as I know."

" St. J. always says there is ' nothing sadder than a happy marriage '."

" Is that why he doesn't risk it himself?"

" I should think Mona will go off with somebody," said Quiggin, decisively.

I considered this comment impertinent, though there was certainly no reason why Quiggin and Templer should be expected to like one another. Perhaps Quiggin's instinct was correct, I thought, however unwilling I might be to agree openly with him. There could be no doubt that the Templers' marriage was not going very well. At the same time, I did not intend to discuss them with Quiggin, to whom, in any case, there seemed no point in explaining Templer's merits. Quiggin would not appreciate these even if they were brought to his notice; while, if it suited him, he would always be ready to reverse his opinion about Templer or anyone else.

By then I had become sceptical of seeing the Isbister introduction, Marxist or otherwise. In itself, this latest suggestion did not strike me as specially surprising. Taking into account the fact that St. John Clarke had made the plunge into " modernism," the project seemed neither more nor less extraordinary than tackling Isbister's pictures from the point of view of Psychoanalysis, Surrealism, Roman Catholicism, Social Credit, or any other specialised approach. In fact some such doctrinal method of attack was then becoming very much the mode; taking the place of the highly coloured critical flights of an earlier generation that still persisted in some quarters, or the severely

technical criticism of the æsthetic puritans who had ruled the roost since the war.

The foreword would now, no doubt, speak of Isbister "laughing up his sleeve" at the rich men and public notabilities he had painted; though Members, who, with St. John Clarke, had once visited Isbister's studio in St. John's Wood for some kind of reception held there, had declared that nothing could have exceeded the painter's obsequiousness to his richer patrons. Members was not always reliable in such matters, but it was certainly true that Isbister's portraits seemed to combine as a rule an effort to flatter his client with apparent attempts to make some comment to be easily understood by the public. Perhaps it was this inward struggle that imparted to his pictures that peculiar fascination to which I have already referred. However, so far as my firm was concerned, the goal was merely to get the introduction written and the book published.

"What is Mark doing now?" I asked.

Quiggin looked surprised at the question; as if everyone must know by now that Members was doing very well for himself.

"With Boggis & Stone—you know they used to be the Vox Populi Press—we got him the job."

"Who were 'we'?"

"St. J. and myself. St. J. arranged most of it through Howard Craggs. As you know, Craggs used to be the managing director of the Vox Populi."

"But I thought Mark wasn't much interested in politics. Aren't all Boggis & Stone's books about Lenin and Trotsky and Litvinov and the Days of October and all that?"

Quiggin agreed with an air of rather forced gaiety.

"Well, haven't most of us been living in a fool's paradise far too long now?" he said, speaking as if to make an

appeal to my better side. "Isn't it time that Mark—and others too—took some notice of what is happening in the world?"

"Does he get a living wage at Boggis & Stone's?"

"With his journalism he can make do. A small firm like that can't afford to pay a very munificent salary, it's true. He still gets a retainer from St. J. for sorting out the books once a month."

I did not imagine this last arrangement was very popular with Quiggin from the way he spoke of it.

"As a matter of fact," he said, "I persuaded St. J. to arrange for Mark to have some sort of a footing in a more politically alive world before he got rid of him. That is where the future lies for all of us."

"Did Gypsy Jones transfer from the Vox Populi to Boggis & Stone?"

Quiggin laughed now with real amusement.

"Oh, no," he said. "I forgot you knew her. She left quite a time before the amalgamation took place. She has something better to do now."

He paused and moistened his lips; adding rather mysteriously:

"They say Gypsy is well looked on by the Party."

This remark did not convey much to me in those days. I was more interested to see how carefully Quiggin's plans must have been laid to have prepared a place for Members even before he had been ejected from his job. That certainly showed forethought.

"Are you writing another book?" said Quiggin.

"Trying to—and you?"

"I liked your first," said Quiggin.

He conveyed by these words a note of warning that, in spite of his modified approval, things must not go too far where books were concerned.

"Personally, I am not too keen to rush into print," he said. "I am still collecting material for my survey, *Unburnt Boats*."

I did not meet Members to hear his side of the story until much later, in fact on that same afternoon of the Isbister Memorial Exhibition. I ran into him on my way through Hyde Park, not far from the Achilles Statue. (As it happened, it was close to the spot where I had come on Barbara Goring and Eleanor Walpole-Wilson, the day we had visited the Albert Memorial together.)

The weather had turned colder again, and the park was dank, with a kind of sea mist veiling the trees. Members looked shabbier than was usual for him: shabby and rather worried. In our undergraduate days he had been a tall, willowy, gesticulating figure, freckled and beady-eyed; hurrying through the lanes and byways of the university, abstractedly alone, like the Scholar-Gypsy, or straggling along the shopfronts of the town in the company of acquaintances, seemingly chosen for their peculiar resemblance to himself. Now he had grown into a terse, emaciated, rather determined young man, with a neat profile and chilly manner: a person people were beginning to know by name. In fact the critics, as a whole, had spoken so highly of his latest volume of verse—the one through which an undercurrent of psychoanalytical phraseology had intermittently run—that even Quiggin (usually as sparing of praise as Uncle Giles himself) had, in one of his more unbending moments at a sherry party, gone so far as to admit publicly:

"Mark has arrived."

As St. John Clarke's secretary, Members had been competent to deal at a moment's notice with most worldly problems. For example, he could cut short the beery protests of some broken-down crony of the novelist's past, ar-

rived unexpectedly on the doorstep—or, to be more precise, on the landing of the block of flats where St. John Clarke lived—with a view to borrowing " a fiver " on the strength of " the old days." Any such former boon companion, if strong-willed, might have got away with " half a sovereign " (as St. John Clarke always called that sum) had he gained entry to the novelist himself. With Members as a buffer, he soon found himself escorted to the lift, having to plan, as he descended, both then and for the future, economic attack elsewhere.

Alternatively, the matter to be regulated might be the behaviour of some great lady, aware that St. John Clarke was a person of a certain limited eminence, but at the same time ignorant of his credentials to celebrity. Again, Members could put right a situation that had gone amiss. Lady Huntercombe must have been guilty of some such social dissonance at her own table (before a secretary had come into existence to adjust such matters by a subsequent word) because Members was fond of quoting a *mot* of his master's to the effect that dinner at the Huntercombes' possessed " only two dramatic features—the wine was a farce and the food a tragedy."

In fact to get rid of a secretary who performed his often difficult functions so effectively was a rash step on the part of a man who liked to be steered painlessly through the shoals and shallows of social life. Indeed, looking back afterwards, the dismissal of Members might almost be regarded as a landmark in the general disintegration of society in its traditional form. It was an act of individual folly on the part of St. John Clarke; a piece of recklessness that well illustrates the mixture of self-assurance and *ennui* which together contributed so much to form the state of mind of people like St. John Clarke at that time. Of course I did

not recognise its broader aspects then. The duel between Members and Quiggin seemed merely an entertaining conflict to watch, rather than the significant crumbling of social foundations.

On that dank afternoon in the park Members had abandoned some of his accustomed coldness of manner. He seemed glad to talk to someone—probably to anyone—about his recent ejection. He began on the subject at once, drawing his tightly-waisted overcoat more closely round him, while he contracted his sharp, beady brown eyes. Separation from St. John Clarke, and association with the firm of Boggis & Stone, had for some reason renewed his former resemblance to an ingeniously constructed marionette or rag doll.

" There had been a slight sense of strain for some months between St. J. and myself," he said. " An absolutely trivial matter about taking a girl out to dinner. Perhaps rather foolishly, I had told St. J. I was going to a lecture on the Little Entente. Howard Craggs—whom I am now working with—happened to be introducing the lecturer, and so of course within twenty-four hours he had managed to mention to St. J. the fact that I had not been present. It was awkward, naturally, but I did not think St. J. really minded.

" But why did you want to know about the Little Entente?"

" St. J. had begun to be rather keen on what he called ' the European Situation '," said Members, brushing aside my surprise as almost impertinent. " I always liked to humour his whims."

" But I thought his great thing was the Ivory Tower?"

" Of course, I found out later that Quiggin had put him up to ' the European Situation '," admitted Members,

grudgingly. " But after all, an artist has certain respon-sibilities. I expect you are a supporter of the League your-self, my dear Nicholas."

He smiled as he uttered the last part of the sentence, though speaking as if he intended to administer a slight, if well deserved, rebuke. In doing this he involuntarily adopted a more personal rendering of Quiggin's own nasal intonation, which rendered quite unnecessary the explana-tion that the idea had been Quiggin's. Probably the very words he used were Quiggin's, too.

" But politics were just what you used to complain of in Quiggin."

" Perhaps Quiggin was right in that respect, if in no other," said Members, giving his tinny, bitter laugh.

" And then?"

" It turned out that St. J.'s feelings *were* rather hurt."

Members paused, as if he did not know how best to set about explaining the situation further. He shook his head once or twice in his old, abstracted Scholar-Gypsy manner. Then he began, as it were, at a new place in his narrative.

" As you probably know," he continued, " I can say with-out boasting that I had done a good deal to change—why should I not say it?—to improve St. J.'s attitude towards intellectual matters. Do you know, when I first came to him he thought Matisse was a *plage*—no, I mean it."

He made no attempt to relax his features, nor join in audible amusement at such a state of affairs. Instead, he continued to record St. John Clarke's shortcomings.

" That much quoted remark of his: ' Gorki is a Rus-sian d'Annunzio '—he got it from me. I happened to say at tea one day that I thought if d'Annunzio had been born in Nijni Novgorod he would have had much the same career as Gorki. All St. J. did was to turn the words round and use them as his own."

" But you still see him from time to time?"

Members shied away his rather distinguished profile like a high-bred but displeased horse.

"Yes—and no," he conceded. "It's rather awkward. I don't know how much Quiggin told you, nor if he spoke the truth."

"He said you came in occasionally to look after the books."

"Only once in a way. I've got to earn a living somehow. Besides, I am attached to St. J.—even after the way he has behaved. I need not tell you that he does not like parting with money. I scarcely get enough for my work on the books to cover my bus fares. It is a strain having to avoid that *âme de boue*, too, whenever I visit the flat. He is usually about somewhere, spying on everyone who crosses the threshold."

"And what about St. John Clarke's conversion to Marxism?"

"When I first persuaded St. J. to look at the world in a contemporary manner," said Members slowly, adopting the tone of one determined not to be hurried in his story by those whose interest in it was actuated only by vulgar curiosity—"When I first persuaded him to that, I took an early opportunity to show him Quiggin. After all, Quiggin was supposed to be my friend—and, whatever one may think of his behaviour as a friend, he has—or had—some talent."

Members waited for my agreement before continuing, as if the thought of displacement by a talentless Quiggin would add additional horror to his own position. I concurred that Quiggin's talent was only too apparent.

" From the very beginning I feared the risk of things going wrong on account of St. J.'s squeamishness about people's personal appearance. For example, I insisted that

Quiggin should put on a clean shirt when he came to see St. J. I told him to attend to his nails. I even gave him an orange stick with which to do so."

" And these preparations were successful?"

" They met once or twice. Quiggin was even asked to the flat. They got on better than I had expected. I admit that. All the same, I never felt that the meetings were really *enjoyable*. I was sorry about that, because I thought Quiggin's ideas would be useful to St. J. I do not always agree with Quiggin's approach to such things as the arts, for example, but he is keenly aware of present-day tendencies. However, I decided in the end to explain to Quiggin that I feared St. J. was not very much taken with him."

" Did Quiggin accept that?"

" He did," said Members, again speaking with bitterness. " He accepted it without a murmur. That, in itself, should have put me on my guard. I know now that almost as soon as I introduced them, they began to see each other when I was not present."

Members checked himself at this point, perhaps feeling that to push his indictment to such lengths bordered on absurdity.

" Of course, there was no particular reason why they should not meet," he allowed. " It was just odd—and rather unfriendly—that neither of them should have mentioned their meetings to me. St. J. always loves new people. ' Unmade friends are like unmade beds,' he has often said. ' They should be attended to early in the morning.' "

Members drew a deep breath that was almost a sigh. There was a pause.

" But I thought you said he was so squeamish about people?"

" Not when he has once decided they are going to be successful."

" That's what he thinks about Quiggin?"

Members nodded.

" Then I noticed St. J. was beginning to describe everything as 'bourgeois'," he said. " Wearing a hat was 'bourgeois', eating pudding with a fork was 'bourgeois', the Ritz was ' bourgeois', Lady Huntercombe was 'bourgeois'—he meant ' bourgeoise', of course, but French is not one of St. J.'s long suits. Then one morning at breakfast he said Cézanne was 'bourgeois'. At first I thought he meant that only middle-class people put too much emphasis on such things—that a true aristocrat could afford to ignore them. It was a favourite theme of St. J.'s that 'natural aristocrats' were the only true ones. He regarded himself as a 'natural aristocrat.' At the same time he felt that a 'natural aristocrat' had a right to mix with the ordinary kind, and latterly he had spent more and more of his time in rather grand circles—and in fact had come almost to hate people who were not rather smart, or at least very rich. For example, I remember him describing—well, I won't say whom, but he is a novelist who sells very well and you can probably guess the name—as ' the kind of man who knows about as much about *placement* as to send the wife of a younger son of a marquess in to dinner before the daughter of an earl married to a commoner.' He thought a lot about such things. That was why I had been at first afraid of introducing him to Quiggin. And then—when we began discussing Cézanne—it turned out that he had been using the word 'bourgeois' all the time in the Marxist sense. I didn't know he had even heard of Marx, much less was at all familiar with his theories."

" I seem to remember an article he wrote describing himself as a 'Gladstonian Liberal'—in fact a Liberal of the most old-fashioned kind."

" You do, you do," said Members, almost passionately.

" I wrote it for him, as a matter of fact. You couldn't have expressed it better. *A Liberal of the most old-fashioned kind*. Local Option—Proportional Representation—Welsh Disestablishment—the whole bag of tricks. That was just about as far as he got. But now everything is ' bourgeois '— Liberalism, I have no doubt, most of all. As a matter of fact, his politics were the only liberal thing about him."

" And it began as soon as he met Quiggin?"

" I first noticed the change when he persuaded me to join in what he called ' collective action on the part of writers and artists '—going to meetings to protest against Manchuria and so on. I agreed, first of all, simply to humour him. It was just as well I did, as a matter of fact, because it led indirectly to another job when he turned his back on me. You know, what St. J. really wants is a son. He wants to be a father without having a wife."

" I thought everyone always tried to avoid that."

" In the Freudian sense," said Members, impatiently, " his nature requires a father-son relationship. Unfortunately, the situation becomes a little too life-like, and one is faced with a kind of artificially constructed Œdipus situation."

" Can't you re-convert him from Marxism to psycho-analysis?"

Members looked at me fixedly.

" St. J. has always pooh-poohed the subconscious," he said.

We were about to move off in our respective directions when my attention was caught by a disturbance coming from the road running within the railings of the park. It was a sound, harsh and grating, though at the same time shrill and suggesting complaint. These were human voices raised in protest. Turning, I saw through the mist that increasingly enveloped the park a column of persons enter-

ing beneath the arch. They trudged behind a mounted policeman, who led their procession about twenty yards ahead. Evidently a political "demonstration" of some sort was on its way to the north side where such meetings were held. From time to time these persons raised a throaty cheer, or an individual voice from amongst them bawled out some form of exhortation. A strident shout, similar to that which had at first drawn my attention, now sounded again. We moved towards the road to obtain a better view.

The front rank consisted of two men in cloth caps, one with a beard, the other wearing dark glasses, who carried between them a banner upon which was inscribed the purpose and location of the gathering. Behind these came some half a dozen personages, marching almost doggedly out of step, as if to deprecate even such a minor element of militarism. At the same time there was a vaguely official air about them. Among these, I thought I recognised the face and figure of a female Member of Parliament whose photograph occasionally appeared in the papers. Next to this woman tramped Sillery. He had exchanged his black soft hat of earlier afternoon for a cloth cap similar to that worn by the bearers of the banner: his walrus moustache and thick strands of white hair blew furiously in the wind. From time to time he clawed at the arm of a gloomy-looking man next to him who walked with a limp. He was grinning all the while to himself, and seemed to be hugely enjoying his role in the procession.

In the throng that straggled several yards behind these more important figures I identified two young men who used to frequent Mr. Deacon's antique shop; one of whom, indeed, was believed to have accompanied Mr. Deacon himself on one of his holidays in Cornwall. I thought, immediately, that Mr. Deacon's other associate, Gypsy Jones,

might also be of the party, but could see no sign of her. Probably, as Quiggin had suggested, she belonged by then to a more distinguished grade of her own hierarchy than that represented by this heterogeneous collection, nearly all apparently " intellectuals " of one kind or another.

However, although interested to see Sillery in such circumstances, there was another far more striking aspect of the procession which a second later riveted my eyes. Members must have taken in this particular spectacle at the same instant as myself, because I heard him beside me give a gasp of irritation.

Three persons immediately followed the group of notables with whom Sillery marched. At first, moving closely together through the mist, this trio seemed like a single grotesque three-headed animal, forming the figurehead of an ornamental car on the roundabout of a fair. As they jolted along, however, their separate entities became revealed, manifesting themselves as a figure in a wheeled chair, jointly pushed by a man and a woman. At first I could not believe my eyes, perhaps even wished to disbelieve them, because I allowed my attention to be distracted for a moment by Sillery's voice shouting in high, almost jocular tones: "Abolish the Means Test!" He had uttered this cry just as he came level with the place where Members and I stood; but he was too occupied with his own concerns to notice us there, although the park was almost empty.

Then I looked again at the three other people, thinking I might find myself mistaken in what I had at first supposed. On the contrary, the earlier impression was correct. The figure in the wheeled chair was St. John Clarke. He was being propelled along the road, in unison, by Quiggin and Mona Templer.

" My God!" said Members, quite quietly.

" Did you see Sillery?"

I asked this because I could think of no suitable comment regarding the more interesting group. Members took no notice of the question.

" I never thought they would go through with it," he said.

Neither St. John Clarke, nor Quiggin wore hats. The novelist's white hair, unenclosed in a cap such as Sillery's was lifted high, like an elderly Struwwelpeter's, in the stiff breeze that was beginning to blow through the branches. Quiggin was dressed in the black leather overcoat he had worn in the Ritz, a red woollen muffler riding up round his neck, his skull cropped like a convict's. No doubt intentionally, he had managed to make himself look like a character from one of the novels of Dostoievski. Mona, too, was hatless, with dishevelled curls: her face very white above a high-necked polo jumper covered by a tweed overcoat of smart cut. She was looking remarkably pretty, and, like Sillery, seemed to be enjoying herself. On the other hand, the features of the two men with her expressed only inexorable sternness. Every few minutes, when the time came for a general shout to be raised, St. John Clarke would brandish in his hand a rolled-up copy of one of the " weeklies," as he yelled the appropriate slogan in a high, excited voice.

" It's an absolute scandal," said Members breathlessly. " I heard rumours that something of the sort was on foot. The strain may easily kill St. J. He ought not to be up— much less taking part in an open-air meeting before the warmer weather comes."

I was myself less surprised at the sight of Quiggin and St. John Clarke in such circumstances than to find Mona teamed up with the pair of them. For Quiggin, this kind of thing had become, after all, almost a matter of routine. It

was " the little political affair " Sillery had mentioned at the private view. St. John Clarke's collaboration in such an outing was equally predictable—apart from the state of his health—after what Members and Quiggin had both said about him. From his acceptance of Quiggin's domination he would henceforward join that group of authors, dons, and clergymen increasingly to be found at that period on political platforms of a " Leftish " sort. To march in some public " demonstration " was an almost unavoidable condition of his new commitments. As it happened he was fortunate enough on this, his first appearance, to find himself in a conveyance. In the wheeled chair, with his long white locks, he made an effective figure, no doubt popular with the organisers and legitimately gratifying to himself.

It was Mona's presence that was at first inexplicable to me. She could hardly have come up for the day to take part in all this. Perhaps the Templers were again in London for the week-end, and she had chosen to walk in the procession as an unusual experience; while Peter had gone off to amuse himself elsewhere. Then all at once the thing came to me in a flash, as such things do, requiring no further explanation. Mona had left Templer. She was now living with Quiggin. For some reason this was absolutely clear. Their relationship was made unmistakable by the manner in which they moved together side by side.

" Where are they going?" I asked.

" To meet some Hunger-Marchers arriving from the Midlands," said Members, as if it were a foolish, irrelevant question. " They are camping in the park, aren't they?"

" This crowd?"

"No, the Hunger-Marchers, of course."

" Why is Mona there?"

" Who is Mona?"

" The girl walking with Quiggin and helping to push

St. John Clarke. She was a model, you remember. I once saw you with her at a party years ago."

" Oh, yes, it was her, wasn't it?" he said, indifferently.

Mona's name seemed to mean nothing to him.

" But why is she helping to push the chair?"

" Probably because Quiggin is too bloody lazy to do all the work himself," he said.

Evidently he was ignorant of Mona's subsequent career since the days when he had known her. The fact that she was helping to trundle St. John Clarke through the mists of Hyde Park was natural enough for the sort of girl she had been. In the eyes of Members she was just another " arty " woman roped in by Quiggin to assist Left Wing activities. His own thoughts were entirely engrossed by St. John Clarke and Quiggin. I could not help being impressed by the extent to which the loss of his post as secretary had upset him. His feelings had undoubtedly been lacerated. He watched them pass by, his mouth clenched.

The procession wound up the road towards Marble Arch. Two policemen on foot brought up the rear, round whom, whistling shrilly, circled some boys on bicycles, apparently unconnected with the marchers. The intermittent shouting grew gradually fainter, until the column disappeared from sight into the still foggy upper reaches of the park.

Members looked round at me.

" Can you beat it?" he said.

" I thought St. John Clarke disliked girls near him?"

" I don't expect he cares any longer," said Members, in a voice of despair. " Quiggin will make him put up with anything by now."

On this note we parted company. As I continued my way through the park I was conscious of having witnessed a spectacle that was distinctly strange. Jean had already told me more than once that the Templers were getting on

badly. These troubles had begun, so it appeared, a few months after their marriage, Mona complaining of the dullness of life away from London. She was for ever making scenes, usually about nothing at all. Afterwards there would be tears and reconciliations; and some sort of a "treat" would be arranged for her by Peter. Then the cycle would once more take its course. Jean liked Mona, but thought her "impossible" as a wife.

"What is the real trouble?" I had asked.

"I don't think she likes men."

"Ah."

"But I don't think she likes women either. Just keen on herself."

"How will it end?"

"They may settle down. If Peter doesn't lose interest. He is used to having his own way. He has been unexpectedly good so far."

She was fond of Peter, though free from that obsessive interest that often entangles brother and sister. They were not alike in appearance, though her hair, too, grew down like his in a "widow's peak" on her forehead. There was also something about the set of her neck that recalled her brother. That was all.

"They might have a lot of children."

"They might."

"Would that be a good thing?"

"Certainly."

I was surprised that she was so decisive, because in those days children were rather out of fashion. It always seemed strange to me, and rather unreal, that so much of her own time should be occupied with Polly.

"You know, I believe Mona has taken quite a fancy for your friend J. G. Quiggin," she had said, laughing.

"Not possible."

" I'm not so sure."

" Has he appeared at the house again?"

" No—but she keeps talking about him."

" Perhaps I ought never to have introduced him into the household."

" Perhaps not," she had replied, quite seriously.

At the time, the suggestion had seemed laughable. To regard Quiggin as a competitor with Templer for a woman —far less his own wife—was ludicrous even to consider.

" But she took scarcely any notice of him."

" Well, I thought *you* were rather wet the first time you came to the house. But I've made up for it later, haven't I?"

" I adored you from the start."

" I'm sure you didn't."

" Certainly at Stourwater."

" Oh, at Stourwater I was very impressed too."

" And I with you."

" Then why didn't you write or ring up or something? *Why didn't you?*"

" I did—you were away."

" You ought to have gone on trying."

" I wasn't sure you weren't rather lesbian."

" How ridiculous. Pretty rude of you, too."

" I had a lot to put up with."

" Nonsense."

" But I had."

" How absurd you are."

When the colour came quickly into her face, the change used to fill me with excitement. Even when she sat in silence, scarcely answering if addressed, such moods seemed a necessary part of her: something not to be utterly regretted. Her forehead, high and white, gave a withdrawn look, like a great lady in a medieval triptych or carving;

only her lips, and the elegantly long lashes under slanting eyes, gave a hint of latent sensuality. But descriptions of a woman's outward appearance can hardly do more than echo the terms of a fashion paper. Their nature can be caught only in a refractive beam, as with light passing through water: the rays of character focused through the person with whom they are intimately associated. Perhaps, therefore, I alone was responsible for what she seemed to me. To another man—Duport, for example—she no doubt appeared—indeed, actually was—a different woman.

" But why, when we first met, did you never talk about books and things?" I had asked her.

" I didn't think you'd understand."

" How hopeless of you."

" Now I see it was," she had said, quite humbly.

She shared with her brother the conviction that she " belonged " in no particular world. The other guests she had found collected round Sir Magnus Donners at Stourwater had been on the whole unsympathetic.

" I only went because I was a friend of Baby's," she had said; " I didn't really like people of that sort."

" But surely there were people of all sorts there?"

" Perhaps I don't much like people anyway. I am probably too lazy. They always want to sleep with one, or something."

" But that is like me."

" I know. It's intolerable."

We laughed, but I had felt the chill of sudden jealousy; the fear that her remark had been made deliberately to tease.

" Of course Baby loves it all," she went on. " The men hum round her like bees. She is so funny with them."

" What did she and Sir Magnus do?"

"Not even I know. Whatever it was, Bijou Ardglass refused to take him on."

"She was offered the job?"

"So I was told. She preferred to go off with Bob."

"Why did that stop?"

"Bob could no longer support her in the style to which she was accustomed—or rather the style to which she was unaccustomed, as Jumbo Ardglass never had much money."

It was impossible, as ever, to tell from her tone what she felt about Duport. I wondered whether she would leave him and marry me. I had not asked her, and had no clear idea what the answer would be. Certainly, if she did, like Lady Ardglass, she would not be supported in the style to which she had been accustomed. Neither, for that matter, would Mona, if she had indeed gone off with Quiggin, for I felt sure that the final domestic upheaval at the Templers' had now taken place. Jean had been right. Something about the way Quiggin and Mona walked beside one another connected them inexorably together. "Women can be immensely obtuse about all kinds of things," Barnby was fond of saying, "but where the emotions are concerned their opinion is always worthy of consideration."

The mist was lifting now, and gleams of sunlight were once more coming through the clouds above the waters of the Serpentine. Not unwillingly dismissing the financial side of marriage from my mind, as I walked on through the melancholy park, I thought of love, which, from the very beginning perpetually changes its shape : sometimes in the ascendant, sometimes in decline. At present we sailed in comparatively calm seas because we lived from meeting to meeting, possessing no plan for the future. Her aban-

donment remained; the abandonment that had so much surprised me at that first embrace, as the car skimmed the muddy surfaces of the Great West Road.

But in love, like everything else—more than anything else—there must be bad as well as good; and by silence or some trivial remark she could inflict unexpected pain. Away from her, all activities seemed waste of time, yet sometimes just before seeing her I was aware of an odd sense of antagonism that had taken the place of the longing that had been in my heart for days before. This sense of being out of key with her sometimes survived the first minutes of our meeting. Then, all at once, tension would be relaxed; always, so it seemed to me, by some mysterious force emanating from her: intangible, invisible, yet at the same time part of a whole principle of behaviour: a deliberate act of the will by which she exercised power. At times it was almost as if she intended me to feel that unexpected accident, rather than a carefully arranged plan, had brought us together on some given occasion; or at least that I must always be prepared for such a mood. Perhaps these are inward irritations always produced by love: the acutely sensitive nerves of intimacy: the haunting fear that all may not go well.

Still thinking of such things, I rang the bell of the ground-floor flat. It was in an old-fashioned red-brick block of buildings, situated somewhere beyond Rutland Gate, concealed among obscure turnings that seemed to lead no-where. For some time there was no answer to the ring. I waited, peering through the frosted glass of the front door, feeling every second an eternity. Then the door opened a few inches and Jean looked out. I saw her face only for a moment. She was laughing.

" Come in," she said quickly. " It's cold."

As I entered the hall, closing the door behind me, she

ran back along the passage. I saw that she wore nothing but a pair of slippers.

"There is a fire in here," she called from the sitting-room.

I hung my hat on the grotesque piece of furniture, designed for that use, that stood by the door. Then I followed her down the passage and into the room. The furniture and decoration of the flat were of an appalling banality.

"Why are you wearing no clothes?"

"Are you shocked?"

"What do you think?"

"I think you are."

"Surprised, rather than shocked."

"To make up for the formality of our last meeting."

"Aren't I showing my appreciation?"

"Yes, but you must not be so conventional."

"But if it had been the postman?"

"I could have seen through the glass."

"He, too, perhaps."

"I had a dressing-gown handy."

"It was a kind thought, anyway."

"You like it?"

"Very much."

"Tell me something nice."

"This style suits you."

"Not too *outré*?"

"On the contrary."

"Is this how you like me?"

"Just like this."

There is, after all, no pleasure like that given by a woman who really wants to see you. Here, at last, was some real escape from the world. The calculated anonymity of the surroundings somehow increased the sense of being alone

with her. There was no sound except her sharp intake of breath. Yet love, for all the escape it offers, is closely linked with everyday things, even with the affairs of others. I knew Jean would burn with curiosity when I told her of the procession in the park. At the same time, because passion in its transcendence cannot be shared with any other element, I could not speak of what had happened until the time had come to decide where to dine.

She was pulling on her stockings when I told her. She gave a little cry, indicating disbelief.

" After all, you were the first to suggest something was ' on ' between them."

" But she would be insane to leave Peter."

We discussed this. The act of marching in a political demonstration did not, in itself, strike her as particularly unexpected in Mona. She said that Mona always longed to take part in anything that drew attention to herself. Jean was unwilling to believe that pushing St. John Clarke's chair was the outward sign of a decisive step in joining Quiggin.

" She must have done it because Peter is away. It is exactly the kind of thing that would appeal to her. Besides, it would annoy him just the right amount. A little, but not too much."

" Where is Peter?"

" Spending the week-end with business friends. Mona thought them too boring to visit."

" Perhaps she was just having a day out, then. Even so, it confirms your view that Quiggin made a hit with her."

She pulled on the other stocking.

" True, they had a splitting row just before Peter left home," she said. " You know, I almost believe you are right."

" Put a call through."

" Just to see what the form is?"

" Why not?"

" Shall I?"

She was undecided.

" I think I will," she said at last.

Still only partly dressed, she took up the telephone and lay on the sofa. At the other end of the line the bell rang for some little time before there was an answer. Then a voice spoke from the Templers' house. Jean made some trivial enquiry. A short conversation followed. I saw from her face that my guess had been somewhere near the mark. She hung up the receiver.

" Mona left the house yesterday, saying she did not know when she would be back. She took a fair amount of luggage and left no address. I think the Burdens believe something is up. Mrs. Burden told me Peter had rung up about something he had forgotten. She told him Mona had left unexpectedly."

" She may be taking a few days off."

" I don't think so," said Jean.

Barnby used to say: "All women are stimulated by the news that any wife has left any husband." Certainly I was aware that the emotional atmosphere in the room had changed. Perhaps I should have waited longer before telling her my story. Yet to postpone the information further was scarcely possible without appearing deliberately secretive. I have often pondered on the conversation that followed, without coming to any definite conclusion as to why things took the course they did.

We had gone on to talk of the week-end when Quiggin had been first invited to the Templers' house. I had remarked something to the effect that if Mona had really left for good, the subject would have been apt for one of Mrs. Erdleigh's prophecies. In saying this I had added some

more or less derogatory remark about Jimmy Stripling.
Suddenly I was aware that Jean was displeased with my
words. Her face took on a look of vexation. I suppose that
some out-of-the-way loyalty had for some reason made her
take exception to the idea of laughing at her sister's ex-hus-
band. I could not imagine why this should be, since Stripling was usually regarded in the Templer household as an
object of almost perpetual derision.

"I know he isn't *intelligent*," she said.

"Intelligence isn't everything," I said, trying to pass the
matter off lightly. "Look at the people in the Cabinet."

"You said the other day that you found it awfully difficult to get on with people who were not intelligent."

"I only meant where writing was concerned."

"It didn't sound like that."

A woman's power of imitation and adaptation make her
capable of confronting you with your own arguments after
even the briefest acquaintance: how much more so if a
state of intimacy exists. I saw that we were about to find
ourselves in deep water. She pursed her lips and looked
away. I thought she was going to cry. I could not imagine
what had gone wrong and began to feel that terrible sense
of exhaustion that descends, when, without cause or warning, an unavoidable, meaningless quarrel develops with
someone you love. Now there seemed no way out. To
lavish excessive praise on Jimmy Stripling's intellectual
attainments would not be accepted, might even seem
satirical; on the other hand, to remain silent would seem
to confirm my undoubtedly low opinion of his capabilities in
that direction. There was also, of course, the more general
implication of her remark, the suggestion of protest against
a state of mind in which intellectual qualities were automatically put first. Dissent from this principle was, after all,
reasonable enough, though not exactly an equitable weapon

in Jean's hands; for she, as much as anyone—so it seemed to me as her lover—was dependent, in the last resort, on people who were " intelligent " in the sense in which she used the word.

Perhaps it was foolish to pursue the point of what was to all appearances only an irritable remark. But the circumstances were of a kind when irritating remarks are particularly to be avoided. Otherwise, it would have been easier to find an excuse.

Often enough, women love the arts and those who practise them; but they possess also a kind of jealousy of those activities. They like wit, but hate analysis. They are always prepared to fall back upon traditional rather than intellectual defensive positions. We never talked of Duport, as I have already recorded, and I scarcely knew, even then, why she had married him; but married they were. Accordingly, it seemed to me possible that what she had said possessed reference, in some oblique manner, to her husband; in the sense that adverse criticism of this kind cast a reflection upon him, and consequently upon herself. I had said nothing of Duport (who, as I was to discover years later, had a deep respect for " intelligence "), but the possibility was something to be taken into account.

I was quite wrong in this surmise, and, even then, did not realise the seriousness of the situation; certainly was wholly unprepared for what happened next. A moment later, for no apparent reason, she told me she had had a love affair with Jimmy Stripling.

" When?"

" After Babs left him," she said.

She went white, as if she might be about to faint. I was myself overcome with a horrible feeling of nausea, as if one had suddenly woken from sleep and found oneself chained to a corpse. A desire to separate myself physically from her

and the place we were in was linked with an overwhelming sensation that, more than ever, I wanted her for myself. To think of her as wife of Bob Duport was bad enough, but that she should have been mistress of Jimmy Stripling was barely endurable. Yet it was hard to know how to frame a complaint regarding that matter even to myself. She had not been " unfaithful " to me. This odious thing had happened at a time when I myself had no claim whatsoever over her. I tried to tranquillise myself by considering whether a liaison with some man, otherwise possible to like or admire, would have been preferable. In the face of such an alternative, I decided Stripling was on the whole better as he was: with all the nightmarish fantasies implicit in the situation. The mystery remained why she should choose that particular moment to reveal this experience of hers, making of it a kind of defiance.

When you are in love with someone, their life, past, present and future, becomes in a curious way part of your life; and yet, at the same time, since two separate human entities in fact remain, you merely carry your own prejudices into another person's imagined existence; not even into their " real " existence, because only they themselves can estimate what their " real " existence has been. Indeed, the situation might be compared with that to be experienced in due course in the army where an officer is responsible for the conduct of troops stationed at a post too distant from him for the exercise of any effective control.

Not only was it painful enough to think of Jean giving herself to another man; the pain was intensified by supposing—what was, of course, not possible—that Stripling must appear to her in the same terms that he appeared to me. Yet clearly she had, once, at least, looked at Stripling with quite different eyes, or such a situation could never have arisen. Therefore, seeing Stripling as a man for whom

it was evidently possible to feel at the very least a passing *tendresse*—perhaps even love—this incident, unforgettably horrible as it seemed to me at the time, would more rationally be regarded as a mere error of judgment. In love, however, there is no rationality. Besides, that she had seen him with other eyes than mine made things worse. In such ways one is bound, inescapably, to the actions of others.

We finished dressing in silence. By that time it was fairly late. I felt at once hungry, and without any true desire for food.

"Where shall we go?"

"Anywhere you like."

"But where would you like to go?"

"I don't care."

"We could have a sandwich at Foppa's."

"The club?"

"Yes."

"All right."

In the street she slipped her arm through mine. I looked, and saw that she was crying a little, but I was no nearer understanding her earlier motives. The only thing clear was that some sharp change had taken place in the kaleidoscope of our connected emotions. In the pattern left by this transmutation of coloured crystals an increased intimacy had possibly emerged. Perhaps that was something she had intended.

"I suppose I should not have told you."

"It would have come out sooner or later."

"But not just then."

"Perhaps not."

Still, in spite of it all, as we drove through dingy Soho streets, her head resting on my shoulder, I felt glad she still seemed to belong to me. Foppa's was open. That was

a relief, for there was sometimes an intermediate period when the restaurant was closed down and the club had not yet come into active being. We climbed the narrow staircase, over which brooded a peculiarly Italian smell: minestrone: salad oil: stale tobacco: perhaps a faint reminder of the lotion Foppa used on his hair.

Barnby had first introduced me to Foppa's club a long time before. One of the merits of the place was that no one either of us knew ever went there. It was a single room over Foppa's Restaurant. In theory the club opened only after the restaurant had shut for the night, but in practice Foppa himself, sometimes feeling understandably bored with his customers, would retire upstairs to read the paper, or practise billiard strokes. On such occasions he was glad of company at an earlier hour than was customary. Alternatively, he would sometimes go off with his friends to another haunt of theirs, leaving a notice on the door, written in indelible pencil, saying that Foppa's Club was temporarily closed for cleaning.

There was a narrow window at the far end of this small, smoky apartment; a bar in one corner, and a table for the game of Russian billiards in the other. The walls were white and bare, the vermouth bottles above the little bar shining out in bright stripes of colour that seemed to form a kind of spectrum in red, white and green. These patriotic colours linked the aperitifs and liqueurs with the portrait of Victor Emmanuel II which hung over the mantelpiece. Surrounded by a wreath of laurel, the King of Sardinia and United Italy wore a wasp-waisted military frock-coat swagged with coils of yellow aiguillette. The bold treatment of his costume by the artist almost suggested a Bakst design for one of the early Russian ballets. If Foppa himself had grown his moustache to the same enormous length, and added an imperial to his chin, he

would have looked remarkably like the *re galantuomo*; with just that same air of royal amusement that anyone could possibly take seriously—even for a moment—the preposterous world in which we are fated to have our being. Hanging over the elaborately gilded frame of this coloured print was the beautiful Miss Foppa's black fez-like cap, which she possessed by virtue of belonging to some local, parochial branch of the Fascist Party; though her father was believed to be at best only a lukewarm supporter of Mussolini's régime. Foppa had lived in London for many years. He had even served as a cook during the war with a British light infantry regiment; but he had never taken out papers of naturalisation.

"Look at me," he used to say, when the subject arose, "I am not an Englishman. You see."

The truth of that assertion was undeniable. Foppa was not an Englishman. He did not usually express political opinions in the presence of his customers, but he had once, quite exceptionally, indicated to me a newspaper photograph of the Duce declaiming from the balcony of the Palazzo Venezia. That was as near as he had ever gone to stating his view. It was sufficient. Merely by varying in no way his habitual expression of tolerant amusement, Foppa had managed to convey his total lack of anything that could possibly be accepted as Fascist enthusiasm. All the same, I think he had no objection to his daughter's association with that or any other party which might be in power at the moment.

Foppa was decidedly short, always exquisitely dressed in a neat blue, or brown, suit, his tiny feet encased in excruciatingly tight shoes of light tan shade. The shoes were sharply pointed and polished to form dazzling highlights. In summer he varied his footgear by sporting white brogues picked out in snakeskin. He was a great gambler,

and sometimes spent his week-ends taking part in trotting races somewhere not far from London, perhaps at Greenford in Middlesex. Hanging behind the bar was a framed photograph of himself competing in one of these trotting events, armed with a long whip, wearing a jockey cap, his small person almost hidden between the tail of his horse and the giant wheels of the sulky. The snapshot recalled a design of Degas or Guys. That was the world, æsthetically speaking, to which Foppa belonged. He was a man of great good nature and independence, who could not curb his taste for gambling for high stakes; a passion that brought him finally, I believe, into difficulties.

Jean and I had already been to the club several times, because she liked playing Russian billiards, a game at which she was extremely proficient. Sixpence in the slot of the table brought to the surface the white balls and the red. After a quarter of an hour the balls no longer reappeared for play, vanishing one by one, while scores were doubled. Foppa approved of Jean. Her skill at billiards was a perpetual surprise and delight to him.

"He probably tells all his friends I'm his mistress," she used to say.

She may have been right in supposing that; though I suspect, if he told any such stories, that Foppa would probably have boasted of some enormous lady, at least twice his own size, conceived in the manner of Jordaens. His turn of humour always suggested something of that sort.

I thought the club might be a good place to recover some sort of composure. The room was never very full, though sometimes there would be a party of three or four playing cards gravely at one of the tables in the corner. On that particular evening Foppa himself was engrossed in a two-handed game, perhaps piquet. Sitting opposite him, his

back to the room, was a man of whom nothing could be seen but a brown check suit and a smoothly brushed head, greying and a trifle bald at the crown. Foppa rose at once, poured out Chianti for us, and shouted down the service hatch for sandwiches to be cut. Although the cook was believed to be a Cypriot, the traditional phrase for attracting his attention was always formulated in French.

" Là bas!" Foppa would intone liturgically, as he leant forward into the abyss that reached down towards the kitchen, " Là bas!"

Perhaps Miss Foppa herself attended to the provision of food in the evenings. If so, she never appeared in the club. Her quiet, melancholy beauty would have ornamented the place. I had, indeed, never seen any woman but Jean in that room. No doubt the clientèle would have objected to the presence there of any lady not entirely removed from their own daily life.

Two Soho Italians were standing by the bar. One, a tall, sallow, mournful character, resembling a former ambassador fallen on evil days, smoked a short, stinking cigar. The other, a nondescript ruffian, smaller in size than his companion, though also with a certain air of authority, displayed a suggestion of side-whisker under his fawn velour hat. He was picking his teeth pensively with one of the toothpicks supplied in tissue paper at the bar. Both were probably neighbouring head-waiters. The two of them watched Jean slide the cue gently between finger and thumb before making her first shot. The ambassadorial one removed the cigar from his mouth and, turning his head a fraction, remarked sententiously through almost closed lips:

" Bella posizione."

" E in gamba," agreed the other. " Una fuori classe davvero."

The evening was happier now, though still something might easily go wrong. There was no certainty. People are differently equipped for withstanding emotional discomfort. On the whole women can bear a good deal of that kind of strain without apparently undue inconvenience. The game was won by Jean.

"What about another one?"

We asked the Italians if they were waiting for the billiard table, but they did not want to play. We had just arranged the balls again, and set up the pin, when the door of the club opened and two people came into the room. One of them was Barnby. The girl with him was known to me, Lady Anne Stepney. We had not met for three years or more. Barnby seemed surprised, perhaps not altogether pleased, to find someone he knew at Foppa's.

Although it had turned out that Anne Stepney was the girl he had met on the train after his week-end with the Manaschs', he had ceased to speak of her freely in conversation. At the same time I knew he was still seeing her. This was on account of a casual word dropped by him. I had never before run across them together in public. Some weeks after his first mention of her, I had asked whether he had finally established her identity. Barnby had replied brusquely:

"Of course her name is Stepney."

I sometimes wondered how the two of them were getting along; even whether they had plans for marriage. A year was a long time for Barnby to be occupied with one woman. Like most men of his temperament, he held, on the whole, rather strict views regarding other people's morals. For that reason alone he would probably not have approved had I told him about Jean. In any case he was not greatly interested in such things unless himself involved. He only knew that something of the sort was in progress, and he

would have had no desire, could it have been avoided, to come upon us unexpectedly in this manner.

The only change in Anne Stepney (last seen at Stringham's wedding) was her adoption of a style of dress implicitly suggesting an art student; nothing outrageous: just a general assertion that she was in some way closely connected with painting or sculpture. I think Mona had struggled against such an appearance; in Anne Stepney, it had no doubt been painfully acquired. Clothes of that sort certainly suited her large dark eyes and reddish hair, seeming also appropriate to a general air of untidiness, not to say grubbiness, that always possessed her. She had by then, I knew, passed almost completely from the world in which she had been brought up; that in which her sister, Peggy, still moved, or, at least, in that portion of it frequented by young married women.

The Bridgnorths had taken their younger daughter's behaviour philosophically. They had gone through all the normal processes of giving her a start in life, a ball for her " coming out," and everything else to be reasonably expected of parents in the circumstances. In the end they had agreed that " in these days " it was impossible to insist on the hopes or standards of their own generation. Anne had been allowed to go her own way, while Lady Bridgnorth had returned to her hospital committees and Lord Bridgnorth to his politics and racing. They had probably contented themselves with the thought that Peggy, having quietly divorced Stringham, had now settled down peacefully enough with her new husband in his haunted, Palladian Yorkshire home, which was said to have given St. John Clarke the background for a novel. Besides, their eldest son, Mountfichet, I had been told, was turning out well at the university, where he was a great favourite with Sillery.

When introductions took place, it seemed simpler to make no reference to the fact that we had met before. Anne Stepney stared round the room with severe approval. Indicating Foppa and his companion, she remarked:

"I always think people playing cards make such a good pattern."

"Rather like a Chardin," I suggested.

"Do you think so?" she replied, implying contradiction rather than agreement.

"The composition?"

"You know I am really only interested in Chardin's highlights," she said.

Before we could pursue the intricacies of Chardin's technique further, Foppa rose to supply further drinks. He had already made a sign of apology at his delay in doing this, to be accounted for by the fact that his game was on the point of completion when Barnby arrived. He now noted the score on a piece of paper and came towards us. He was followed this time to the bar by the man with whom he had been at cards. Foppa's companion could now be seen more clearly. His suit was better cut and general appearance more distinguished than was usual in the club. He had stood by the table for a moment, stretching himself and lighting a cigarette, while he regarded our group. A moment later, taking a step towards Anne Stepney, he said in a soft, purring, rather humorous voice, with something almost hypnotic about its tone:

"I heard your name when you were introduced. You must be Eddie Bridgnorth's daughter."

Looking at him more closely as he said this, I was surprised that he had remained almost unobserved until that moment. He was no ordinary person. That was clear. Of medium height, even rather small when not compared with Foppa, he was slim, with that indefinably "horsey" look

that seems even to affect the texture of the skin. His age was hard to guess: probably he was in his forties. He was very trim in his clothes. They were old, neat, well preserved clothes, a little like those worn by Uncle Giles. This man gave the impression of having handled large sums of money in his time, although he did not convey any presumption of affluence at that particular moment. He was clean-shaven, and wore a hard collar and Brigade of Guards tie. I could not imagine what someone of that sort was doing at Foppa's. There was something about him of Buster Foxe, third husband of Stringham's mother: the same cool, tough, socially elegant personality, though far more genial than Buster's. He lacked, too, that carapace of professional egotism acquired in boyhood that envelops protectively even the most good-humoured naval officer. Perhaps the similarity to Buster was after all only the outer veneer acquired by all people of the same generation.

Anne Stepney replied rather stiffly to this enquiry, that "Eddie Bridgnorth" was indeed her father. Having decided to throw in her lot so uncompromisingly with "artists," she may have felt put out to find herself confronted in such a place by someone of this kind. Since he claimed acquaintance with Lord Bridgnorth, there was no knowing what information he might possess about herself; nor what he might report subsequently if he saw her father again. However, the man in the Guards tie seemed instinctively to understand what her feelings would be on learning that he knew her family.

"I am Dicky Umfraville," he said. "I don't expect you have ever heard of me, because I have been away from this country for so long. I used to see something of your father when he owned Yellow Jack. In fact I won a whole heap of money on that horse once. None of it left now, I regret to say."

He smiled gently. By the confidence, and at the same time the modesty, of his manner he managed to impart an extraordinary sense of reassurance. Anne Stepney seemed hardly to know what to say in answer to this account of himself. I remembered hearing Sillery speak of Umfraville, when I was an undergraduate. Perhaps facetiously, he had told Stringham that Umfraville was a man to beware of. That had been apropos of Stringham's father, and life in Kenya. Stringham himself had met Umfraville in Kenya, and spoke of him as a well-known gentleman-rider. I also remembered Stringham complaining that Le Bas had once mistaken him for Umfraville, who had been at Le Bas's house at least fifteen years earlier. Now, in spite of the difference in age and appearance, I could see that Le Bas's error had been due to something more than the habitual vagueness of schoolmasters. The similarity between Stringham and Umfraville was of a moral rather than physical sort. The same dissatisfaction with life and basic melancholy gave a resemblance, though Unfraville's features and expression were more formalised and, in some manner, coarser—perhaps they could even be called more brutal—than Stringham's.

There was something else about Umfraville that struck me, a characteristic I had noticed in other people of his age. He seemed still young, a person like oneself; and yet at the same time his appearance and manner proclaimed that he had had time to live at least a few years of his grown-up life before the outbreak of war in 1914. Once I had thought of those who had known the epoch of my own childhood as "older people." Then I had found there existed people like Umfraville who seemed somehow to span the gap. They partook of both eras, specially forming the tone of the post-war years; much more so, indeed, than the younger people. Most of them, like Umfraville, were

melancholy; perhaps from the strain of living simultaneously in two different historical periods. That was his
category, certainly. He continued now to address himself
to Anne Stepney.

" Do you ever go to trotting races?"

" No."

She looked very surprised at the question.

" I thought not," he said, laughing at her astonishment.
" I became interested when I was in the States. The
Yanks are very keen on trotting races. So are the French.
In this country no one much ever seems to go. However,
I met Foppa, here, down at Greenford the other day and
we got on so well that we arranged to go to Caversham to-
gether. The next thing is I find myself playing piquet with
him in his own joint."

Foppa laughed at this account of the birth of their friendship, and rubbed his hands together.

" You had all the luck to-night, Mr. Umfraville," he said.
" Next time I have my revenge."

" Certainly, Foppa, certainly."

However, in spite of the way the cards had fallen, Foppa
seemed pleased to have Umfraville in the club. Later, I
found that one of Umfraville's most fortunate gifts was a
capacity to take money off people without causing offence.

A moment or two of general conversation followed in
which it turned out that Jean had met Barnby on one of
his visits to Stourwater. She knew, of course, about his
former connection with Baby Wentworth, but when we
had talked of this together, she had been uncertain whether
or not they had ever stayed with Sir Magnus Donners at
the same time. They began to discuss the week-end during
which they had both been in the same large house-party.
Anne Stepney, possibly to avoid a further immediate impact with Umfraville before deciding on how best to treat

him, crossed the room to examine Victor Emmanuel's picture. Umfraville and I were, accordingly, left together. I asked if he remembered Stringham in Kenya.

"Charles Stringham?" he said. "Yes, of course I knew him. Boffles Stringham's son. A very nice boy. But wasn't he married to *her* sister?"

He lowered his voice, and jerked his head in Anne's direction.

"They are divorced now."

"Of course they are. I forgot. As a matter of fact I heard Charles was in rather a bad way. Drinking enough to float a battleship. Of course, Boffles likes his liquor hard, too. Have you known Charles long?"

"We were at the same house at school—Le Bas's."

"Not possible."

"Why not?"

"Because I was at Le Bas's too. Not for very long. I started at Corderey's. Then Corderey's house was taken over by Le Bas. I was asked to leave quite soon after that—not actually sacked, as is sometimes maliciously stated by my friends. I get invited to Old Boy dinners, for example. Not that I ever go. Usually out of England. As a matter of fact I might go this year. What about you?"

"I might. I haven't been myself for a year or two."

"Do come. We'll make up a party and raise hell. Tear Claridge's in half. That's where they hold it, isn't it?"

"Or the Ritz."

"You must come."

There was a suggestion of madness in the way he shot out his sentences; not the kind of madness that was raving, nor even, in the ordinary sense, dangerous; but a warning that no proper mechanism existed for operating normal controls. At the same time there was also something im-

pelling about his friendliness: this sudden decision that we must attend the Old Boy dinner together. Even though I knew fairly well—at least flattered myself I knew well—the type of man he was, I could not help being pleased by the invitation. Certainly, I made up my mind immediately that I would go to the Le Bas dinner, upon which I was far from decided before. In fact, it would be true to say that Umfraville had completely won me over; no doubt by the shock tactics against which Sillery had issued his original warning. In such matters, though he might often talk nonsense, Sillery possessed a strong foundation of shrewdness. People who disregarded his admonitions sometimes lived to regret it.

" Do you often come here?" Umfraville asked.

" Once in a way—to play Russian billiards."

" Tell me the name of that other charming girl."

" Jean Duport."

" Anything to do with the fellow who keeps company with Bijou Ardglass?"

" Wife."

" Dear me. How eccentric of him with something so nice at home. Anne, over there, is a dear little thing, too. Bit of a handful, I hear. Fancy her being grown up. Only seems the other day I read the announcement of her birth. Wouldn't mind taking her out to dinner one day, if I had the price of a dinner on me."

" Do you live permanently in Kenya?"

" Did for a time. Got rather tired of it lately. Isn't what it was in the early days. But, you know, something seems to have gone badly wrong with this country too. It's quite different from when I was over here two or three years ago. Then there was a party every night—two or three, as a matter of fact. Now all that is changed. No parties, no

gaiety, everyone talking in a dreadfully serious manner about economics or world disarmament or something of the sort. That was why I was glad to come here and take a hand with Foppa. No nonsense about economics or world disarmament with him. All the people I know have become so damned serious, what? Don't you find that yourself?"

" It's the slump."

Umfraville's face had taken on a strained, worried expression while he was saying this, almost the countenance of a priest preaching a gospel of pleasure to a congregation now fallen away from the high standards of the past. There was a look of hopelessness in his eyes, as if he knew of the terrible odds against him, and the martyrdom that would be his final crown. At that moment he again reminded me, for some reason, of Buster Foxe. I had never heard Buster express such opinions, though in general they were at that time voiced commonly enough. " Anyway, it's nice to find all of you here," he said. " Let's have another drink."

Barnby and Anne Stepney now began to play billiards together. They seemed not on the best of terms, and had perhaps had some sort of a quarrel earlier in the evening. If Mrs. Erdleigh had been able to examine the astrological potentialities of that day she would perhaps have warned groups of lovers that the aspects were ominous. Jean came across to the bar. She took my arm, as if she wished to emphasise to Umfraville that we were on the closest terms. This was in spite of the fact that she herself was always advocating discretion. All the same, I felt delighted and warmed by her touch. Umfraville smiled, almost paternally, as if he felt that here at least he could detect on our part some hope of a pursuit of pleasure. He showed no disposition to return to his game with Foppa, now chatting with the two Italians.

" Charles Stringham was mixed up with Milly Andriadis at one moment, wasn't he?" Umfraville asked.

" About three years ago—just before his marriage."

" I think it was just starting when I was last in London. Don't expect that really did him any good. Milly has got a way of exhausting chaps, no matter who they are. Even her Crowned Heads. They can't stand it after a bit. I remember one friend of mine had to take a voyage round the world to recover. He got D.T.s in Hongkong. Thought he was being hunted by naked women riding on unicorns. What's happened to Milly now?"

" I only met her once—at a party Charles took me to."

" Why don't we all go and see her?"

" I don't think any of us really know her."

" But *I* couldn't know her better."

" Where does she live?"

" Where's the telephone book?" said Umfraville. " Though I don't expect she will be in England at this time of year."

He moved away, lost in thought, and disappeared through the door. It occurred to me that he was pretty drunk, but at the same time I was not sure. Equally possible was the supposition that this was his first drink of the evening. The mystery surrounded him that belongs especially to strong characters who have only pottered about in life. Jean slipped her hand in mine.

" Who is he?"

I tried to explain to her who Umfraville was.

" I am enjoying myself," she said.

" Are you?"

I could not be quite sure whether I was enjoying myself or not. We watched the other two playing billiards. The game was evidently war to the knife. They were evenly matched. There could be no doubt now that there had been

some sort of disagreement between them before their arrival at Foppa's. Perhaps all girls were in a difficult mood that night.

" I've often heard of Umfraville," said Barnby, chalking his cue. "Didn't he take two women to St. Moritz one year, and get fed up with them, and left them there to pay the hotel bill?"

" Who is he married to now?" Anne Stepney asked.

" Free as air at the moment, I believe," said Barnby. " He has had several wives—three at least. One of them poisoned herself. Another left him for a marquess—and almost immediately eloped again with a jockey. What happened to the third I can't remember. Your shot, my dear."

Umfraville returned to the room. He watched the completion of the game in silence. It was won by Barnby. Then he spoke.

" I have a proposition to make," he said. " I got on to Milly Andriadis just now on the telephone and told her we were all coming round to see her."

My first thought was that I could not make a habit of arriving with a gang of friends at Mrs. Andriadis's house as an uninvited guest; even at intervals of three or four years. A moment later I saw the absurdity of such diffidence, because, apart from any other consideration, she would not have the faintest remembrance of ever having met me before. At the same time, I could not inwardly disregard the pattern of life which caused Dicky Umfraville not only to resemble Stringham, but also, by this vicarious invitation, to re-enact Stringham's past behaviour.

" What is this suggestion?" inquired Anne Stepney.

She spoke coldly, but I think Umfraville had already thoroughly aroused her interest. At any rate her eyes reflected that rather puzzled look that in women is some-

times the prelude to an inclination for the man on whom it is directed.

"Someone called Mrs. Andriadis," said Umfraville. "She has been giving parties since you were so high. Rather a famous lady. A very old friend of mine. I thought we might go round and see her. I rang her up just now and she can't wait to welcome us."

"Oh, do let's go," said Anne Stepney, suddenly abandoning her bored, listless tone. "I've always longed to meet Mrs. Andriadis. Wasn't she some king's mistress— was it——"

"It was," said Umfraville.

"I've heard so many stories of the wonderful parties she gives."

Umfraville stepped forward and took her hand. "Your ladyship wishes to come," he said softly, as if playing the part of a courtier in some ludicrously mannered ceremonial. "We go, then. Yours to command."

He bent his head over the tips of her fingers. I could not see whether his lips actually touched them, but the burlesque was for some reason extraordinarily funny, so that we all laughed. Yet, although absurd, Umfraville's gesture had also a kind of grace which clearly pleased and flattered Anne Stepney. She even blushed a little. Although he laughed with the rest of us, I saw that Barnby was a trifle put out, as indeed most men would have been in the circumstances. He had certainly recognised Umfraville as a rival with a technique entirely different from his own. I looked across to Jean to see if she wanted to join the expedition. She nodded quickly and smiled. All at once things were going all right again between us.

"I've only met Mrs. Andriadis a couple of times," said Barnby. "But we got on very well on both occasions—in

fact she bought a drawing. I suppose she won't mind such a large crowd?"

"Mind?" said Umfraville. "My dear old boy, Milly will be tickled to death. Come along. We can all squeeze into one taxi. Foppa, we shall meet again. You shall have your revenge."

Mrs. Andriadis was, of course, no longer living in the Duports' house in Hill Street, where Stringham had taken me to the party. That house had been sold by Duport at the time of his financial disaster. She was now installed, so it appeared, in a large block of flats recently erected in Park Lane. I was curious to see how her circumstances would strike me on re-examination. Her party had seemed, at the time, to reveal a new and fascinating form of life, which one might never experience again. Such a world now was not only far less remarkable than formerly, but also its special characteristics appeared scarcely necessary to seek in an active manner. Its elements had, indeed, grown up all round one like strange tropical vegetation: more luxuriant, it was true, in some directions rather than others: attractive here, repellent there, but along every track that could be followed almost equally dense and imprisoning.

"She really said she would like to see us?" I asked, as, tightly packed, we ascended in the lift.

Umfraville's reply was less assuring than might have been hoped.

"She said, 'Oh, God, you again, Dicky. Somebody told me you died of drink in 1929.' I said, 'Milly, I'm coming straight round with a few friends to give you that kiss I forgot when we were in Havana together.' She said, 'Well, I hope you'll bring along that pony you owe me, too, which you forgot at the same time.' So saying, she snapped the receiver down."

" So she has no idea how many we are?"

" Milly knows I have lots of friends."

" All the same——"

" Don't worry, old boy. Milly will eat you all up. Especially as you are a friend of Charles."

I was on the contrary, not at all sure that it would be wise to mention Stringham's name to Mrs. Andriadis.

" We had to sue her after she took our house," said Jean.

" Yes, I expect so," said Umfraville.

The circumstances of our arrival did not seem specially favourable in the light of these remarks. We were admitted to what was evidently a large flat by an elderly lady's-maid, who had the anxious, authoritative demeanour of a nanny, or nursery governess, long established in the family.

" Well, Ethel," said Umfraville. " How are you keeping? Quite a long time since we met."

Her face brightened at once when she recognised him.

" And how are *you*, Mr. Umfraville? Haven't set eyes on you since the days in Cuba. You look very well indeed, sir. Where did you get your sunburn?"

" Not too bad, Ethel. What a time it was in Cuba. And how is Mrs. A.?"

" She's been a bit poorly, sir, on and off. Not quite her own old self. She has her ups and downs."

" Which of us doesn't, Ethel? Will she be glad to see me?"

It seemed rather late in the day to make this enquiry. Ethel's reply was not immediate. Her face contracted a trifle as she concentrated her attention upon an entirely truthful answer to this delicate question.

" She was pleased when you rang up," she said. " Very pleased. Called me in and told me, just as she would have

done in the old days. But then Mr. Guggenbühl telephoned just after you did, and after that I don't know that she was so keen. She's changeable, you know. Always was."

" Mr. Guggenbühl is the latest, is he?"

Ethel laughed, with the easy good manners of a trusted servant whose tact is infinite. She made no attempt to indicate the identity of Mr. Guggenbühl.

" What's he like?" Umfraville asked, wheedling in his manner.

" He's a German gentleman, sir."

" Old, young? Rich, poor?"

" He's quite young, sir. Shouldn't say he was specially wealthy."

" One of that kind, is he?" said Umfraville. " Everybody seems to have a German boy these days. I feel quite out of fashion not to have one in tow myself. Does he live here?"

" Stays sometimes."

" Well, we won't remain long," said Umfraville. " I quite understand."

We followed him through a door, opened by Ethel, which led into a luxurious rather than comfortable room. There was an impression of heavy damask curtains and fringed chair-covers. Furniture and decoration had evidently been designed in one piece, little or nothing having been added to the original scheme by the present owner. A few books and magazines lying on a low table in Chinese Chippendale seemed strangely out of place; even more so, a model theatre, like a child's, which stood on a Louis XVI commode.

Mrs. Andriadis herself was lying in an arm-chair, her legs resting on a pouf. Her features had not changed at all from the time when I had last seen her. Her powder-grey hair remained beautifully trim; her dark eyebrows still

arched over very bright brown eyes. She looked as pretty as before, and as full of energy. She wore no jewellery except a huge square cut diamond on one finger.

Her clothes, on the other hand, had undergone a strange alteration. Her small body was now enveloped in a black cloak, its velvet collar clipped together at the neck by a short chain of metal links. The garment suggested an Italian officer's uniform cloak, which it probably was. Beneath this military outer covering was a suit of grey flannel pyjamas, mean in design and much too big for her; in fact obviously intended for a man. One trouser leg was rucked up, showing her slim calf and ankle. She did not rise, but made a movement with her hand to show that she desired us all to find a place to sit.

"Well, Dicky," she said, "why the hell do you want to bring a crowd of people to see me at this time of night?"

She spoke dryly, though without bad temper, in that distinctly cockney drawl that I remembered.

"Milly, darling, they are all the most charming people imaginable. Let me tell you who they are."

Mrs. Andriadis laughed.

"I know *him*," she said nodding in the direction of Barnby.

"Lady Anne Stepney," said Umfraville. "Do you remember when we went in her father's party to the St. Leger?"

"You'd better not say anything about *that*," said Mrs. Andriadis. "Eddie Bridgnorth has become a pillar of respectability. How is your sister, Anne? I'm not surprised she had to leave Charles Stringham. Such a charmer, but no woman could stay married to him for long."

Anne Stepney looked rather taken aback at this peremptory approach.

"And Mrs. Duport," said Umfraville.

" Was it your house I took in Hill Street?"

" Yes," said Jean, " it was."

I wondered whether there would be an explosion at this disclosure. The trouble at the house had involved some question of a broken looking-glass and a burnt-out boiler. Perhaps there had been other items too. Certainly there had been a great deal of unpleasantness. However, in the unexpected manner of persons who live their lives at a furious rate, Mrs. Andriadis merely said in a subdued voice :

" You know, my dear, I want to apologise for all that happened in that wretched house. If I told you the whole story, you would agree that I was not altogether to blame. But it is all much too boring to go into now. At least you got your money. I hope it really paid for the damage."

" We've got rid of the house now," Jean said, laughing. " I didn't ever like it much anyway."

" And Mr. Jenkins," Umfraville said. " A friend of Charles's——"

She gave me a keen look.

" I believe I've seen you before too," she said.

I hoped she was not going to recall the scene Mr. Deacon had made at her party. However, she carried the matter no further.

" Ethel," she shouted, " bring some glasses. There is beer for those who can't drink whisky."

She turned towards Umfraville.

" I'm quite glad to see you all," she said; " but you mustn't stay too long after Werner appears. He doesn't approve of people like you."

" Your latest beau, Milly?"

" Werner Guggenbühl. Such a charming German boy. He will be terribly tired when he arrives. He has been walking in a procession all day."

" To meet the Hunger-Marchers?" I asked.

It had suddenly struck me that in the complicated pattern life forms, this visit to Mrs. Andriadis was all part of the same diagram as that in which St. John Clarke, Quiggin and Mona had played their part that afternoon.

" I think so. Were you marching too?"

" No—but I knew some people who were."

" What an extraordinary world we live in," said Umfraville. " All one's friends marching about in the park."

" Rather sweet of Werner, don't you agree?" said Mrs. Andriadis. " Considering this isn't his own country and all the awful things we did to Germany at the Versailles Treaty."

Before she could say more about him, Guggenbühl himself arrived in the room. He was dark and not bad-looking in a very German style. His irritable expression recalled Quiggin's. He bowed slightly from the waist when introduced, but took no notice of any individual, not even Mrs. Andriadis herself, merely glancing round the room and then glaring straight ahead of him. There could be no doubt that he was the owner of the grey pyjamas. He reminded me of a friend of Mr. Deacon's called " Willi:" described by Mr. Deacon as having " borne much of the heat of the day over against Verdun when nation rose against nation." Guggenbühl was a bit younger than Willi, but in character they might easily have a good deal in common.

" What sort of a day did you have, Werner?" asked Mrs. Andriadis.

She used a coaxing voice, quite unlike the manner in which she had spoken up to that moment. The tone made me think of Templer trying to appease Mona. It was equally unavailing, for Guggenbühl made an angry gesture with his fist.

" What was it like, you ask," he said. " So it was like everything in this country. Social-Democratic antics. Of it let us not speak."

He turned away in the direction of the model theatre. Taking no further notice of us, he began to manipulate the scenery, or play about in some other manner with the equipment at the back of the stage.

" Werner is writing a play," explained Mrs. Andriadis, speaking now in a much more placatory manner. " We sometimes run through the First Act in the evening. How is it going, Werner?"

" Oh, are you?" said Anne Stepney. " I'm terribly interested in the Theatre. Do tell us what it is about."

Guggenbühl turned his head at this.

" I think it would not interest you," he said. " We have done with old theatre of bourgeoisie and capitalists. Here is *Volksbühnen*—for actor that is worker like industrial worker—actor that is machine of machines."

" Isn't it too thrilling?" said Mrs. Andriadis. " You know the October Revolution was the real turning point in the history of the Theatre."

" Oh, I'm sure it was," said Anne Stepney. " I've read a lot about the Moscow Art Theatre."

Guggenbühl made a hissing sound with his lips, expressing considerable contempt.

" Moscow Art Theatre is just to tolerate," he said, " but what of biomechanics, of *Trümmer-Kunst*, has it? Then Shakespeare's *Ein Sommernachtstraum* or Toller's *Masse-Mensch* will you take? The modern ethico-social play I think you do not like. Hauptmann, Kaiser, plays to Rosa Luxemburg and Karl Liebknecht, yes. The new corporate life. The socially conscious form. Drama as highest of arts we Germans know. No mere entertainment, please. *Lebensstimmung* it is. But it is workers untouched by middle

class that will make spontaneous. Of Moscow Art Theatre you speak. So there was founded at Revolution both Theatre and Art Soviet, millions, billions of roubles set aside by Moscow Soviet of Soldier Deputies. Hundreds, thousands of persons. Actors, singers, clowns, dancers, musicians, craftsmen, designers, mechanics, electricians, scene-shifters, all kinds of manual workers, all trained, yes, and supplying themselves to make. Two years to have one perfect single production—if needed so, three, four, five, ten years. At other time, fifty plays on fifty successive nights. It is not be getting money, no."

His cold, hard voice, offering instruction, stopped abruptly.

" Any ventriloquists?" Umfraville asked.

The remark passed unnoticed, because Anne Stepney broke in again.

" I can't think why we don't have a revolution here," she said, " and start something of that sort."

" You would have a revolution here?" said Guggenbühl, smiling rather grimly. " So? Then I am in agreement with you."

" Werner thinks the time has come to act," said Mrs. Andriadis, returning to her more decisive manner. " He says we have been talking for too long."

" Oh, I do agree," said Anne Stepney.

I asked Guggenbühl if he had come across St. John Clarke that afternoon. At this question his manner at once changed.

" You know him? The writer."

" I know the man and the girl who were pushing him."

" Ach, so."

He seemed uncertain what line to take about St. John Clarke. Perhaps he was displeased with himself for having made disparaging remarks about the procession in

front of someone who knew two of the participants and might report his words.

" He is a famous author, I think."

" Quite well known."

" He ask me to visit him."

" Are you going?"

" Of course."

" Did you meet Quiggin—his secretary—my friend?"

" I think he goes away soon to get married."

" To the girl he was with?"

" I think so. Mr. Clarke ask me to visit him when your friend is gone for some weeks. He says he will be lonely and would like to talk."

Probably feeling that he had wasted enough time already with the company assembled in the room, and at the same time being unwilling to give too much away to someone he did not know, Guggenbühl returned, after saying this, to the model theatre. Ostentatiously, he continued to play about with its accessories. We drank our beer. Even Umfraville seemed a little put out of countenance by Guggenbühl, who had certainly brought an atmosphere of peculiar unfriendliness and disquiet into the room. Mrs. Andriadis herself perhaps took some pleasure in the general discomfiture for which he was responsible. The imposition of one kind of a guest upon another is a form of exercising power that appeals to most persons who have devoted a good deal of their life to entertaining. Mrs. Andriadis, as a hostess of long standing and varied experience, was probably no exception. In addition to that, she, like St. John Clarke, had evidently succumbed recently to a political conversion, using Guggenbühl as her vehicle. His uncompromising behaviour no doubt expressed to perfection the role to which he was assigned in her mind : the scourge of frivolous persons of the sort she knew so well.

However, one of the essential gifts of an accomplished hostess is an ability to dismiss, quietly and speedily, guests who have overstayed their welcome. Mrs. Andriadis must have possessed this ingenuity to an unusual degree. I can remember no details of how our party was shifted. Perhaps Umfraville made a movement to go that was quickly accepted. Brief good-byes were said. One way or another, in an unbelievably short space of time, we found ourselves once more in Park Lane.

" You see," said Umfraville. " Even Milly . . ."

Some sort of a discussion followed as to whether or not the evening should be brought to a close at this point. Umfraville and Anne Stepney were unwilling to go home; Barnby was uncertain what he wanted to do; Jean and I agreed that we had had enough. The end of it was that the other two decided to accompany Umfraville to a place where a " last drink " could be obtained. Other people's behaviour seemed unimportant to me; for in some way the day had righted itself, and once more the two of us seemed close together.

FIVE

When, in describing Widmerpool's new employment, Templer had spoken of " the Acceptance World," I had been struck by the phrase. Even as a technical definition, it seemed to suggest what we are all doing; not only in business, but in love, art, religion, philosophy, politics, in fact all human activities. The Acceptance World was the world in which the essential element—happiness, for example—is drawn, as it were, from an engagement to meet a bill. Sometimes the goods are delivered, even a small profit made; sometimes the goods are not delivered, and disaster follows; sometimes the goods are delivered, but the value of the currency is changed. Besides, in another sense, the whole world is the Acceptance World as one approaches thirty; at least some illusions discarded. The mere fact of still existing as a human being proved that.

I did not see Templer himself until later in the summer, when I attended the Old Boy Dinner for members of Le Bas's house. That year the dinner was held at the Ritz. We met in one of the subterranean passages leading to the private room where we were to eat. It was a warm, rather stuffy July evening. Templer, like a Frenchman, wore a white waistcoat with his dinner-jacket, a fashion of the moment: perhaps by then already a little outmoded.

" We always seem to meet in these gorgeous halls," he said.

" We do."

" I expect you've heard that Mona bolted," he went on

quickly. " Joined up with that friend of yours of the remarkable suit and strong political views."

His voice was casual, but it had a note of obsession as if his nerves were on edge. His appearance was unchanged; possibly a little thinner.

Mona's elopement had certainly been discussed widely. In the break-up of a marriage the world inclines to take the side of the partner with most vitality, rather than the one apparently least to blame. In the Templers' case public opinion had turned out unexpectedly favourable to Mona; probably because Templer himself was unknown to most of the people who talked to me of the matter. Normal inaccuracies of gossip were increased by this ignorance. In one version, Mona was represented as immensely rich, ill treated by an elderly, unsuccessful stockbroker; another described Templer as unable to fulfil a husband's role from physical dislike of women. A third account included a twenty-minute hand-to-hand struggle between the two men, at the end of which Quiggin had gained the victory: a narrative sometimes varied to a form in which Templer beat Quiggin unconscious with a shooting-stick. In a different vein was yet another story describing Templer, infatuated with his secretary, paying Quiggin a large sum to take Mona off his hands.

On the whole people are unwilling to understand even comparatively simple situations where husband and wife are concerned; indeed, a simple explanation is the last thing ever acceptable. Here, certainly, was something complicated enough; a striking reversal of what might be thought the ordinary course of events. Templer, a man undoubtedly attractive to women, loses his wife to Quiggin, a man usually ill at ease in women's company: Mona, as Anna Karenin, directing her romantic feelings towards Karenin as a lover, rather than Vronsky as a husband. For

me, the irony was emphasised by Templer being my first schoolboy friend to seem perfectly at home with the opposite sex; indeed, the first to have practical experience in that quarter. But conflict between the sexes might be compared with the engagement of boxers in which the best style is not always victorious.

"What will they live on?" Templer said. "Mona is quite an expensive luxury in her way."

I had wondered that, too, especially in the light of an experience of a few weeks before, when in the Café Royal with Barnby. In those days there was a female orchestra raised on a dais at one side of the huge room where you had drinks. They were playing *In a Persian Market*, and in that noisy, crowded, glaring, for some reason rather ominous atmosphere, which seemed specially designed to hear such confidences, Barnby had been telling me that matters were at an end between Anne Stepney and himself. That had not specially surprised me after the evening at Foppa's. Barnby had reached the climax of his story when Quiggin and Mark Members passed our table, side by side, on their way to the diners' end of the room. That was, to say the least, unexpected. They appeared to be on perfectly friendly terms with each other. When they saw us, Members had given a distant, evasive smile, but Quiggin stopped to speak. He seemed in an excellent humour.

"How are you, Nick?"

"All right."

"Mark and I are going to celebrate the completion of *Unburnt Boats*," he said. "It is a wonderful thing to finish a book."

"When is it to appear?"

"Autumn."

I felt sure Quiggin had stopped like this in order to make some statement that would define more clearly his

own position. That would certainly be a reasonable aim on his part. I was curious to know why the two of them were friends again; also to learn what was happening about Quiggin and Mona. Such information as I then possessed had come from Jean, who knew from her brother only that they had gone abroad together. At the same time, as a friend of Templer's, I did not want to appear too obviously willing to condone the fact that Quiggin had eloped with his wife.

"Mona and I are in Sussex now," said Quiggin, in a voice that could almost be described as unctuous, so much did it avoid his usual harsh note. "We have been lent a cottage. I am just up for the night to see Mark and make final arrangements with my publisher."

He talked as if he had been married to Mona, or at least lived with her, for years; just as, a few months earlier, he had spoken as if he had always been St. John Clarke's secretary. It seemed hard to do anything but accept the relationship as a *fait accompli*. Such things have to be.

"Can you deal with St. John Clarke from so far away?"

"How do you mean?"

Quiggin's face clouded, taking on an expression suggesting he had heard the name of St. John Clarke, but was quite unable to place its associations.

"Aren't you still his secretary?"

"Oh, good gracious, no," said Quiggin, unable to repress a laugh at the idea.

"I hadn't heard you'd left him."

"But he has become a Trotskyist."

"What form does it take?"

Quiggin laughed again. He evidently wished to show his complete agreement that the situation regarding St. John Clarke was so preposterous that only a certain degree of

jocularity could carry it off. Laughter, his manner indicated, was a more civilised reaction than the savage rage that would have been the natural emotion of most right-minded persons on hearing the news for the first time.

" The chief form," he said, " is that he consequently now requires a secretary who is also a Trotskyist."

"Who has he got?"

"You would not know him."

"Someone beyond the pale?"

" He has found a young German to pander to him, as a matter of fact. One Guggenbühl."

" I have met him as a matter of fact."

"Have you?" said Quiggin, without interest. "Then I should advise you to steer clear of Trotskyists in the future, if I were you."

"Was this very sudden?"

" My own departure was not entirely involuntary," said Quiggin. " At first I thought the man would rise above the difficulties of my domestic situation. I—and Mona, too—did everything to assist and humour him. In the end it was no good."

He had moved off then, at the same time gathering in Members, who had been chatting to a girl in dark glasses sitting at a neighbouring table.

" We shall stay in the country until the divorce comes through," he had said over his shoulder.

The story going round was that Mona had been introduced by Quiggin to St. John Clarke as a political sympathiser. Only later had the novelist discovered the story of her close association with Quiggin. He had begun to make difficulties at once. Quiggin, seeing that circumstances prevented the continuance of his job, made a goodish bargain with St. John Clarke, and departed. Guggenbühl must have stepped into the vacuum. No one seemed

to know the precise moment when he had taken Quiggin's place; nor how matters remained regarding Mrs. Andriadis.

Like Templer, I wondered how Quiggin and Mona would make two ends meet, but these details could hardly be gone into then and there in the Ritz.

" I suppose Quiggin keeps afloat," I said. " For one thing, he must have just had an advance for his book. Still, I don't expect that was anything colossal."

" That aunt of Mona's died the other day," said Templer. " She left Mona her savings—a thousand or so, I think."

" So they won't starve."

" As a matter of fact I haven't cut her allowance yet," he said, reddening slightly. " I suppose one will have to in due course."

He paused.

" I must say it was the hell of a surprise," he said. " We'd had plenty of rows, but I certainly never thought she would go off with a chap who looked quite so like something the cat had brought in."

I could only laugh and agree. These things are capable of no real explanation. Mona's behaviour was perhaps to be examined in the light of her exalted feelings for Quiggin as a literary figure. Combined with this was, no doubt, a kind of envy of her husband's former successes with other women; for such successes with the opposite sex put him, as it were, in direct competition with herself. It is, after all, envy rather than jealousy that causes most of the trouble in married life.

" I've really come here to-night to see Widmerpool," said Templer, as if he wished to change the subject. " Bob Duport is in England again. I think I told you Widmerpool might help him land on his feet."

I felt a sense of uneasiness that he found it natural to tell me this. Jean had always insisted that her brother knew

nothing of the two of us. Probably she was right; though I could never be sure that someone with such highly developed instincts where relations between the sexes were concerned could remain entirely unaware that his sister was having a love affair. On the other hand he never saw us together. No doubt, so far as Jean was concerned, he would have regarded a lover as only natural in her situation. He was an exception to the general rule that made Barnby, for example, puritanically disapproving of an irregular life in others. In any case, he probably spoke of Duport in the way people so often do in such circumstances, ignorant of the facts, yet moved by some unconscious inner process to link significant names together. All the same, I was conscious of a feeling of foreboding. I was going to see Jean that night; after the dinner was at an end.

" I am rather hopeful things will be patched up with Jean, if Bob's business gets into running order again," Templer said. " The whole family can't be in a permanent state of being deserted by their husbands and wives. I gather Bob is no longer sleeping with Bijou Ardglass, which was the real cause of the trouble I think."

" Prince Theodoric's girl friend?"

" That's the one. Started life as a mannequin. Then married Ardglass as his second wife. When he died the title, and nearly all the money, went to a distant cousin, so she had to earn a living somehow. Still, it was inconvenient she should have picked on Bob."

By this time we had reached the ante-room where Le Bas's Old Boys were assembling. Le Bas himself had not yet arrived, but Whitney, Maiden, Simson, Brandreth, Ghika, and Fettiplace-Jones were standing about, sipping drinks, and chatting uneasily. All of them, except Ghika, were already showing signs of the wear and tear of life. Whitney was all but unrecognisable with a moustache;

Maiden had taken to spectacles; Simson was prematurely bald; Fettiplace-Jones, who was talking to Widmerpool without much show of enjoyment, although he still looked like a distinguished undergraduate, had developed that ingratiating, almost cringing manner that some politicians assume to avoid an appearance of thrusting themselves forward. Fettiplace-Jones had been Captain of the House when I had arrived there as a new boy and had left at the end of that term. He was now Member of Parliament for some northern constituency.

Several others came in behind Templer and myself. Soon the room became fairly crowded. Most of the new arrivals were older or younger than my own period, so that I knew them only by sight from previous dinners. As it happened, I had not attended a Le Bas dinner for some little time. I hardly knew why I was there that year, for it was exceptional for an old friend like Templer to turn up. I think I had a subdued curiosity to see if Dicky Umfraville would put in an appearance, and fulfil his promise to "tear the place in half." A chance meeting with Maiden, one of the organisers had settled it, and I came. Maiden now buttonholed Templer, and, at the same moment, Fettiplace-Jones moved away from Widmerpool to speak with Simson, who was said to be doing well at the Bar. I found Widmerpool beside me.

" Why, hullo—hullo—Nicholas——" he said.

He glared through his thick glasses, the side pieces of which were becoming increasingly embedded in wedges of fat below his temples. At the same time he transmitted one of those skull-like smiles of conventional friendliness to be generally associated with conviviality of a political sort. He was getting steadily fatter. His dinner-jacket no longer fitted him : perhaps had never done so with much success. Yet he carried this unhappy garment with more of an air

than he would have achieved in the old days; certainly
with more of an air than he had ever worn the famous
overcoat for which he had been notorious at school.

We had met once or twice, always by chance, during the
previous few years. On each occasion he had been going
abroad for the Donners-Brebner Company. "Doing pretty
well," he had always remarked, when asked how things
were with him. His small eyes had glistened behind his
spectacles when he had said this. There was no reason to
disbelieve in his success, though I suspected at the time
that his job might be more splendid in his own eyes than
when regarded by some City figure like Templer. However, after Templer's more recent treatment of him, I supposed that I must be wrong in presuming exaggeration on
Widmerpool's part. Although two or three years older
than myself, he could still be little more than thirty. No
doubt he was "doing well." With the self-confidence he
had developed, he moved now with a kind of strut, a curious adaptation of that uneasy, rubber-shod tread, squeak-
ing rhythmically down the interminable linoleum of our
schooldays. I remembered how Barbara Goring (whom
we had both been in love with, and now I had not thought
of for years) had once poured sugar over his head at a
dance. She would hardly do that to-day. Yet Widmerpool
had never entirely overcome his innate oddness; one might
almost say, his monstrosity. In that he resembled Quiggin.
Perhaps it was the determination of each to live by the will
alone. At any rate, you noticed Widmerpool immediately
upon entering a room. That would have given him satisfaction.

"Do you know, I nearly forgot your Christian name,"
he said, not without geniality. "I have so many things
to remember these days. I was just telling Fettiplace-Jones

about North Africa. In my opinion we should hand back Gibraltar to Spain, taking Ceuta in exchange. Fettiplace-Jones was in general agreement. He belongs to a group in Parliament particularly interested in foreign affairs. I have just come back from those parts."

"For Donners-Brebner?"

He nodded, puffing out his lips and assuming the appearance of a huge fish.

"But not in the future," he said, breathing inward hard. "I'm changing my trade."

"I heard rumours."

"Of what?"

"That you were joining the Acceptance World."

"That's one way of putting it."

Widmerpool sniggered.

"And you?" he asked.

"Nothing much."

"Still producing your art books? It was art books, wasn't it?"

"Yes—and I wrote a book myself."

"Indeed, Nicholas. What sort of a book?"

"A novel, Kenneth."

"Has it been published?"

"A few months ago."

"Oh."

His ignorance of novels and what happened about them was evidently profound. That was, after all, reasonable enough. Perhaps it was just lack of interest on his part. Whatever the cause, he looked not altogether approving, and did not enquire the name of the book. However, probably feeling a moment later that his reply may have sounded a shade flat, he added: "Good . . . good," rather in the manner of Le Bas himself, when faced with an

activity of which he was uninformed and suspicious, though at the same time unjustified in categorically forbidding.

"As a matter of fact I am making some notes for a book myself," said Widmerpool. "Quite a different sort of book from yours, of course. So we may be authors together. Do you always come to these dinners? I have been abroad, or otherwise prevented, on a number of occasions, and thought I would see what had happened to everybody. One sometimes makes useful contacts in such ways."

Le Bas himself arrived in the room at that moment, bursting through the door tumultuously, exactly as if he were about to surprise the party assembled there at some improper activity. It was in this explosive way that he had moved about the house at school. For a second he made me feel as if I were back again under his surveillance; and one young man, with very fair hair, whose name I did not know, went scarlet in the face at his former housemaster's threatening impetuosity, just as if he himself had a guilty conscience.

However, Le Bas, as it turned out, was in an excellent humour. He went round the room shaking hands with everyone, making some comment to each of us, more often than not hopelessly inappropriate, showing that he had mistaken the Old Boy's name or generation. In spite of that I was aware of a feeling of warmth towards him that I had never felt when at school; perhaps because he seemed to represent, like a landscape or building, memories of a vanished time. He had become, if not history, at least part of one's autobiography. In his infinitely ancient dinner-jacket and frayed tie he looked, as usual, wholly unchanged. His clothes were as old as Sillery's, though far better cut. Tall, curiously Teutonic in appearance, still rubbing his

red, seemingly chronically sore eyes, as from time to time he removed his rimless glasses, he came at last to the end of the diners, who had raggedly formed up in line round the room, as if some vestige of school discipline was reborn in them at the appearance of their housemaster. After the final handshake, he took up one of those painful, almost tortured positions habitually affected by him, this particular one seeming to indicate that he had just landed on his heels in the sand after making the long jump.

Maiden, who, as I have said, was one of the organisers of the dinner, and was in the margarine business, now began fussing, as if he thought that by his personal exertions alone would anyone get anything to eat that night. He came up to me, muttering agitatedly.

" Another of your contemporaries accepted—Stringham," he said. " I suppose you don't know if he is turning up? We really ought to go into dinner soon. Should we wait for him? It is really too bad of people to be late for this sort of occasion."

He spoke as if I, or at least all my generation, were responsible for the delay. The news that Stringham might be coming to the dinner surprised me. I asked Maiden about his acceptance of the invitation.

" He doesn't turn up as a rule," Maiden explained, " but I ran into him the other night at the Silver Slipper and he promised to come. He said he would attend if he were sober enough by Friday. He wrote down the time and place on a menu and put it in his pocket. What do you think?"

" I should think we had better go in."

Maiden nodded, and screwed up his yellowish, worried face, which seemed to have taken on sympathetic colouring from the commodity he marketed. I remembered him as a

small boy, perpetually preoccupied with the fear that he would be late for school or games: this tyranny of Time evidently pursuing him no less in later life. Finally, his efforts caused us to troop into the room where we were to dine. From what I had heard of Stringham recently, I thought his appearance at such a dinner extremely unlikely.

At the dinner table I found myself between Templer and a figure who always turned up at these dinners whose name I did not know: a middle-aged—even elderly, he then seemed—grey-moustached man. I had, rather half-heartedly, tried to keep a place next to me for Stringham, but gave up the idea when this person diffidently asked if he might occupy the chair. There were, in any case, some spare places at the end of the table, where Stringham could sit, if he arrived, as a certain amount of latitude always existed regarding the size of the party. It was to be presumed that the man with the grey moustache had been at Corderey's, in the days before Le Bas took over the house; if so, he was the sole survivor from that period who ever put in an appearance. I remembered Maiden had once commented to me on the fact that one of Corderey's Old Boys always turned up, although no one knew him. He had seemed perfectly happy before dinner, drinking a glass of sherry by himself. Hitherto, he had made no effort whatever to talk to any of the rest of the party. Le Bas had greeted him, rather unenthusiastically, with the words " Hullo, Tolland;" but Le Bas was so notoriously vague regarding nomenclature that this name could be accepted only after corroboration. Something about his demeanour reminded me of Uncle Giles, though this man was, of course, considerably younger. There had been a Tolland at school with me, but I had known him only by sight. I asked Templer whether he had any news of Mrs. Erdleigh and Jimmy Stripling.

" I think she is fairly skinning Jimmy," he said, laughing. " They are still hard at it. I saw Jimmy the other day in Pimm's."

The time having come round for another tea at the Ufford, I myself had visited Uncle Giles fairly recently. While there I had enquired, perhaps unwisely, about Mrs. Erdleigh. The question had been prompted partly by curiosity as to what his side of the story might be, partly from an inescapable though rather morbid interest in what happened to Stripling. I should have known better than to have been surprised by the look of complete incomprehension that came over Uncle Giles's face. It was similar technique, though put into more absolute execution, that Quiggin had used when asked about St. John Clarke. No doubt it would have been better to have left the matter of Mrs. Erdleigh alone. I should have known from the start that interrogation would be unproductive.

" Mrs. Erdleigh?"

He had spoken not only as if he had never heard of Mrs. Erdleigh but as if even the name itself could not possibly belong to anyone he had ever encountered.

" The lady who told our fortunes."

" What fortunes?"

" When I was last here."

" Can't understand what you're driving at."

" I met her at tea when I last came here—Mrs. Erdleigh."

" Believe there was someone of that name staying here."

" She came in and you introduced me."

" Rather an actressy woman, wasn't she? Didn't stay very long. Always talking about her troubles, so far as I can remember. Hadn't she been married to a Yangtze pilot, or was that another lady? There was a bit of a fuss about the bill, I believe. Interested in fortune-telling, was she? How did you discover that?"

"She put the cards out for us."

"Never felt very keen about all that fortune-telling stuff," said Uncle Giles, not unkindly. "Doesn't do the nerves any good, in my opinion. Rotten lot of people, most of them, who take it up."

Obviously the subject was to be carried no further. Perhaps Mrs. Erdleigh, to use a favourite phrase of my uncle's, had "let him down." Evidently she herself had been removed from his life as neatly as if by a surgical operation, and, by this mysterious process of voluntary oblivion, was excluded even from his very consciousness; all done, no doubt, by an effort of will. Possibly everyone could live equally untrammelled lives with the same determination. However, this mention of Uncle Giles is by the way.

"Jimmy is an extraordinary fellow," said Templer, as if pondering my question. "I can't imagine why Babs married him. All the same, he is more successful with the girls than you might think."

Before he could elaborate this theme, his train of thought, rather to my relief, was interrupted. The cause of this was the sudden arrival of Stringham. He looked horribly pale, and, although showing no obvious sign of intoxication, I suspected that he had already had a lot to drink. His eyes were glazed, and, holding himself very erect, he walked with the slow dignity of one who is not absolutely sure what is going on round him. He went straight up to the head of the table where Le Bas was sitting and apologised for his lateness—the first course was being cleared—returning down the room to occupy the spare chair beside Ghika at the other end.

"Charles looks as if he has been hitting the martinis pretty hard," said Templer.

I agreed. After a consultation with the wine waiter, Stringham ordered a bottle of champagne. Since Ghika

had already provided himself with a whisky and soda there was evidently no question of splitting it with his next-door neighbour. Templer commented on this to me, and laughed. He seemed to have obtained relief from having discussed the collapse of his marriage with a friend who knew something of the circumstances. He was more cheerful now and spoke of his plans for selling the house near Maidenhead. We began to talk of things that had happened at school.

"Do you remember when Charles arranged for Le Bas to be arrested by the police?" said Templer. "The Braddock alias Thorne affair."

We were sitting too far away from Le Bas for this remark to be overheard by him. Templer looked across to where Stringham was sitting and caught his eye. He jerked his head in Le Bas's direction and held his own wrists together as if he wore handcuffs. Stringham seemed to understand his meaning at once. His face brightened, and he made as if to catch Ghika by the collar. This action had to be explained to Ghika, and, during the interlude, Parkinson, who was on Templer's far side, engaged him in conversation about the Test Match.

I turned to the man with the grey moustache. He seemed to be expecting an approach of some sort, because, before I had time to speak, he said:

"I'm Tolland."

"You were at Corderey's, weren't you?"

"Yes, I was. Seems a long time ago now."

"Did you stay on into Le Bas's time?"

"No. Just missed him."

He was infinitely melancholy; gentle in manner, but with a suggestion of force behind this sad kindliness.

"Was Umfraville there in your time?"

"R. H. J. Umfraville?"

G

"I think so. He's called 'Dicky'."

Tolland gave a slow smile.

"We overlapped," he admitted.

There was a pause.

"Umfraville was my fag," said Tolland, as if drawing the fact from somewhere very deep down within him. "At least I believe he was. I was quite a bit higher up in the school, of course, so I don't remember him very well."

A terrible depression seemed to seize him at the thought of this great seniority of his to Umfraville. There was a lack of serenity about Tolland at close quarters, quite different from the manner in which he had carried off his own loneliness in a crowd. I felt rather uneasy at the thought of having to deal with him, perhaps for the rest of dinner. Whitney was on the other side and there was absolutely no hope of his lending a hand in a case of that sort.

"Umfraville a friend of yours?" asked Tolland.

He spoke almost as if he were condoling with me.

"I've just met him. He said he might be coming to-night."

Tolland looked at me absently. I thought it might be better to abandon the subject of Umfraville. However, a moment or two later he himself returned to it.

"I don't think Umfraville will come to-night," he said. "I heard he'd just got married."

It certainly seemed unlikely that even Umfraville would turn up for dinner at this late stage in the meal, though the reason given was unexpected, even scriptural. Tolland now seemed to regret having volunteered the information.

"Who did he marry?"

This question discomposed him even further. He cleared his throat several times and took a gulp of claret, nearly choking himself.

"As a matter of fact I believe she is a distant cousin of

mine—perhaps not," he said. "I can never remember that sort of thing—yes, she is, though. Of course she is."

"Yes?"

"One of the Bridgnorth girls—Anne, I think."

"Anne Stepney?"

"Yes, yes. That's the one. You probably know her."

"I do."

"Thought you would."

"But she is years younger."

"She is a bit younger. Yes, she is a bit younger. Quite a bit younger. And he has been married before, of course."

"It makes his fourth wife, doesn't it?"

"Yes, I believe it does. His fourth wife. Pretty sure it does make his fourth."

Tolland looked at me in absolute despair, I think not so much at the predicament in which Anne Stepney had involved herself, as at the necessity for such enormities to emerge in conversation. The news was certainly unforeseen.

"What do the Bridgnorths think about it?"

It was perhaps heartless to press him on such a point, but, having been told something so extraordinary as this, I wanted to hear as much as possible about the circumstances. Rather unexpectedly, he seemed almost relieved to report on that aspect of the marriage.

"The fellow who told me in the Guards' Club said they were making the best of it."

"There was no announcement?"

"They were married in Paris," said Tolland. "So this fellow in the Guards' Club—or was it Arthur's?—told me. My brother, Warminster, when he was alive, used to talk about Umfraville. I think he liked him. Perhaps he didn't. But I think he did."

"I was at school with a Tolland."

" My nephew. Did you know his brother, Erridge?
Erridge has succeeded now. Funny boy."

Sir Gavin Walpole-Wilson had mentioned a " Norah
Tolland " as friend of his daughter, Eleanor. She turned
out to be a niece.

" Warminster had ten children. Big family for these
days."

We rose at that moment to drink the King's health; and
Le Bas's. Then Le Bas stood up, gripping the table with
both hands as if he proposed to overturn it. This was in
preparation for the delivery of his accustomed speech, which
varied hardly at all year by year. His guttural, carefully
enunciated consonants echoed through the room.

" . . . cannot fail to be gratifying to see so many of my
former pupils here to-night . . . do not really know what
to say to you all . . . certainly shall not make a long speech
. . . these annual meetings have their importance . . . encourage a sense of continuity . . . give perhaps an opportunity of taking stock . . . friendship . . . I've said to some
of you before . . . needs keeping up . . . probably remember, most of you, lines quoted by me on earlier occasions . . .

> And I sat by the shelf till I lost myself,
> And roamed in a crowded mist,
> And heard lost voices and saw lost looks,
> As I pored on an old School List.

. . . . verses not, of course, in the modern manner . . . some
of us do not find such appeals to sentiment very sympathetic . . . typically Victorian in their emphasis . . . all
the . . . rather well describe what most of us—well—at least
some of us—may—feel—experience—when we meet and
talk over our . . . ."

Here Le Bas, as usual, paused; probably from the convic-

tion that the word " schooldays " had accumulated various
associations in the minds of his listeners to which he was
unwilling to seem to appeal. The use of hackneyed words
had always been one of his preoccupations. He was, I
think, dimly aware that his own bearing was somewhat
clerical, and was accordingly particularly anxious to avoid
the appearance of preaching a sermon. He compromised
at last with " . . . other times . . ." returning, almost immediately, to the poem; as if the increased asperity that
the lines now assumed would purge him from the im-
putation of sentimentality to which he had referred. He
cleared his throat harshly.

" . . . You will remember how it goes later . . .

> There were several duffers and several bores,
>   Whose faces I've half forgot,
> Whom I lived among, when the world was young
>   And who talked no end of rot;

. . . of course I do not mean to suggest that there was anyone like that at my house . . ."

This comment always caused a certain amount of mild
laughter and applause. That evening Whitney uttered some
sort of a cry reminiscent of the hunting field, and Widmerpool grinned and drummed on the tablecloth with his fork,
slightly shaking his head at the same time to indicate that
he did not concur with Le Bas in supposing his former
pupils entirely free from such failings.

" . . . certainly nobody of that sort here to-night . . . but
at the same time . . . no good pretending that all time spent
at school was—entirely blissful . . . certainly not for a
housemaster . . ."

There was more restrained laughter. Le Bas's voice tailed
away. In his accustomed manner he had evidently tried to

steer clear of any suggestion that schooldays were the happiest period of a man's life, but at the same time feared that by tacking too much he might become enmeshed in dangerous admissions from which escape could be difficult. This had always been one of his main anxieties as a schoolmaster. He would go some distance along a path indicated by common sense, but, overcome by caution, would stop half-way and behave in an unexpected, illogical manner. Most of the conflicts between himself and individual boys could be traced to these hesitations at the last moment. Now he paused, beginning again in more rapid sentences:

" . . . as I have already said . . . do not intend to make a long, prosy after-dinner speech . . . nothing more boring . . . in fact my intention is—as at previous dinners—to ask some of you to say a word or two about your own activities since we last met together . . . For example, perhaps Fettiplace-Jones might tell us something of what is going forward in the House of Commons . . ."

Fettiplace-Jones did not need much pressing to oblige in this request. He was on his feet almost before Le Bas had finished speaking. He was a tall, dark, rather good-looking fellow, with a lock of hair that fell from time to time over a high forehead, giving him the appearance of a Victorian statesman in early life. His maiden speech (tearing Ramsay MacDonald into shreds) had made some impression on the House, but since then there had been little if any brilliance about his subsequent parliamentary performances, though he was said to work hard in committee. India's eventual independence was the subject he chose to tell us about, and he continued for some little time. He was followed by Simson, a keen Territorial, who asked for recruits. Widmerpool broke into Simson's speech with more than one " hear, hear." I remembered that he had told me he too

was a Territorial officer. Whitney had something to say of
Tanganyika. Others followed with their appointed piece.
At last they came to an end. It seemed that Le Bas had
exhausted the number of his former pupils from whom he
might hope to extract interesting or improving comment.
Stringham was sitting well back in his chair. He had, I
think, actually gone to sleep.

There was a low buzz of talking. I had begun to
wonder how soon the party would break up, when there
came the sound of someone rising to their feet. It was
Widmerpool. He was standing up in his place, looking
down towards the table, as he fiddled with his glass. He
gave a kind of introductory grunt.

" You have heard something of politics and India," he
said, speaking quickly, and not very intelligibly, in that
thick, irritable voice which I remembered so well. " You
have been asked to join the Territorial Army, an invitation
I most heartily endorse. Something has been said of
county cricket. We have been taken as far afield as the
Congo Basin, and as near home as this very hotel, where
one of us here to-night worked as a waiter while acquiring
his managerial training. Now I—I myself—would like to
say a word or two about my experiences in the City."

Widmerpool stopped speaking for a moment and took a
sip of water. During dinner he had shared a bottle of
Graves with Maiden. There could be no question that he
was absolutely sober. Le Bas—indeed everyone present—
was obviously taken aback by this sudden, uncomfortable
diversion. Le Bas had never liked Widmerpool, and, since
the party was given for Le Bas, and Le Bas had not asked
Widmerpool to speak, this behaviour was certainly uncalled
for. In fact it was unprecedented. There was, of course,
no cogent reason, apart from that, why Widmerpool should
not get up and talk about the life he was leading. Just as

other speakers had done. Indeed, it could be argued that the general invitation to speak put forward by Le Bas required acceptance as a matter of good manners. Perhaps that was how Widmerpool looked at it, assuming that Le Bas had only led off with several individual names as an encouragement for others to take the initiative in describing their lives. All that was true. Yet, in some mysterious manner, school rules, rather than those of the outer world, governed that particular assembly. However successful Widmerpool might have become in his own eyes, he was not yet important in the eyes of those present. He remained a nonentity, perhaps even an oddity, remembered only because he had once worn the wrong sort of overcoat. His behaviour seemed all the more outrageous on account of the ease with which, at that moment on account of the special circumstances, he could force us to listen to him without protest.

" This is terrific," Templer muttered.

I looked across at Stringham, who had now woken up, and, having finished his bottle, was drinking brandy. He did not smile back at me, instead twisting his face into one of those extraordinary resemblances to Widmerpool at which he had always excelled. Almost immediately he resumed his natural expression, still without smiling. The effect of the grimace was so startling that I nearly laughed aloud. At the same time, something set, rather horrifying, about Stringham's own features, put an abrupt end to this sudden spasm of amusement. This look of his even made me feel apprehension as to what Stringham himself might do next. Obviously he was intensely, if quietly, drunk.

Meanwhile, Widmerpool was getting into his stride :

" . . . tell you something of the inner workings of the Donners-Brebner Company," he was saying in a somewhat steadier voice than that in which he had begun his address.

"There is not a man of you, I can safely say, who would not be in a stronger position to face the world if he had some past experience of employment in a big concern of that sort. However, several of you already know that I am turning my attention to rather different spheres. Indeed, I have spoken to some of you of these changes in my life when we have met in the City . . ."

He looked round the room and allowed his eyes to rest for a moment on Templer, smiling again that skull-like grin with which he had greeted us.

"This is getting embarrassing," said Templer.

I think Templer had begun to feel he had too easily allowed himself to accept Widmerpool as a serious person. It was impossible to guess what Widmerpool was going to say next. He was drunk with his own self-importance.

" . . . at one time these financial activities were devoted to the satisfaction of man's greed. Now we have a rather different end in view. We have been suffering—it is true to say that we are still suffering and shall suffer for no little time—from the most devastating trade depression in our recorded history. We have been forced from the Gold Standard, so it seems to me, and others not unworthy of a public hearing, because of the insufficiency of money in the hands of consumers. Very well. I suggest to you that our contemporary anxieties are not entirely vested in the question of balance of payment, that is at least so far as current account may be concerned, and I put it to you that certain persons, who should perhaps have known better, have been responsible for unhappy, indeed catastrophic capital movements through a reckless and inadmissible lending policy."

I had a sudden memory of Monsieur Dubuisson talking like this when Widmerpool and I had been at La Grenadière together.

" . . . where our troubles began," said Widmerpool.

" Now if we have a curve drawn on a piece of paper representing an average ratio of persistence, you will agree that authentic development must be demonstrated by a register alternately ascending and descending the level of our original curve of homogeneous development. Such an image, or, if you prefer it, such a geometrical figure, is dialectically implied precisely by the notion, in itself, of an average ratio of progress. No one would deny that. Now if a governmental policy of regulating domestic prices is to be arrived at in this or any other country, the moment assigned to the compilation of the index number which will establish the par of interest and prices must obviously be that at which internal economic conditions are in a condition of relative equilibrium. So far so good. I need not remind you that the universally accepted process in connection with everyday commodities is for their production to be systematised by the relation between their market value and the practicability of producing them, a steep ascent in value in contrast with the decreased practicability of production proportionately stimulating, and a parallel descent correspondingly depressing production. All that is clear enough. The fact that the index number remains at par regardless of alterations in the comparative prices of marketable commodities included in it, necessarily expresses the unavoidable truth that ascent or descent of a specific commodity is compensated by analogous adjustments in the opposite direction in prices of residual commodities . . ."

How long Widmerpool would have continued to speak on these subjects, it is impossible to say. I think he had settled down in his own mind to make a lengthy speech, whether anyone else present liked it or not. Why he had decided to address the table in this manner was not clear to me. Possibly, he merely desired to rehearse aloud certain economic views of his own, expressing them before an in-

different, even comparatively hostile audience, so that he might judge what minor adjustments ought to be made when the speech was delivered on some far more important occasion. Such an action would not be out of keeping with the eccentric, dogged manner in which he ran his life. At the same time, it was also likely enough that he wanted to impress Le Bas's Old Boys—those former schoolfellows who had so greatly disregarded him—with the fact that he was getting on in the world in spite of them; that he had already become a person to be reckoned with.

Widmerpool may not even have been conscious of this motive, feeling it only instinctively; for there could be no doubt that he now thought of his schooldays in very different terms from any that his contemporaries would have used. Indeed, such references as he had ever made to his time at school, for example when we had been in France together, always suggested that he saw himself as a boy rather above the average at work and games. That justice had never been done to his energies in either direction was on account of the unsatisfactory manner in which both these sides of life were administered by those in authority. Widmerpool had once said this to me in so many words.

The effect of his discourse on those sitting round the table had been mixed. Fettiplace-Jones's long, handsome, pasty face assumed a serious, even worried expression, implying neither agreement nor disagreement with what was being said : merely a public indication that, as a Member of Parliament, he was missing nothing. It was as if he were waiting for the Whip's notification of which way he should vote. Parkinson gave a kind of groan of boredom, which I heard distinctly, although he was separated from me by Templer. Tolland, on the other hand, leant forward as if

he feared to miss a syllable. Simson looked very stern.
Whitney and Brandreth had begun a whispered conversation together. Maiden, who was next to Widmerpool, was
throwing anxious, almost distracted glances about him.
Ghika, like Tolland, leant forward. He fixed his huge
black eyes on Widmerpool, concentrating absolutely on his
words, but whether with interest, or boredom of an intensity that might lead even to physical assault, it was impossible to say. Templer had sat back in his chair, clearly
enjoying every phrase to the full. Stringham also expressed
his appreciation, though only by the faintest smile, as if he
saw all through a cloud. Then, suddenly, the scene was
brought abruptly to a close.

"Look at Le Bas," said Templer.

"It's a stroke," said Tolland.

Afterwards—I mean weeks or months afterwards, when
I happened upon any of the party then present, or heard
the incident discussed—there was facetious comment suggesting that Le Bas's disabling attack had been directly
brought about by Widmerpool's speech. Certainly no one
was in a position categorically to deny that there was no
connection whatever between Widmerpool's conduct and
Le Bas's case. Knowing Le Bas, I have no doubt that he
was sitting in his chair, bitterly regretting that he was no
longer in a position to order Widmerpool to sit down at
once. That would have been natural enough. A sudden
pang of impotent rage may even have contributed to
other elements in bringing on his seizure. But that was
to take rather a melodramatic view. More probably, the
atmosphere of the room, full of cigar smoke and fumes of
food and wine, had been too much for him. Besides, the
weather had grown distinctly hotter as the night wore on.
Le Bas himself had always been a great opener of windows.
He would insist on plenty of fresh air on the coldest winter

day at early school in any room in which he was teaching. His ordinary life had not accustomed him to gatherings of this sort, which he only had to face once a year. No doubt he had always been an abstemious man, in spite of Templer's theory, held at school, that our housemaster was a secret drinker. That night he had possibly taken more wine than he was accustomed. He was by then getting on in years, though no more than in his sixties. The precise cause of his collapse was never known to me. These various elements probably all played a part.

Lying back in his chair, his cheeks flushed and eyes closed, one side of Le Bas's face was slightly contorted. Fettiplace-Jones and Maiden must have taken in the situation at once, because I had scarcely turned in Le Bas's direction before these two had picked him up and carried him into the next room. Widmerpool followed close behind them. There was some confusion when people rose from the table. I followed the rest through the door to the anteroom, where Le Bas was placed full-length on the settee. Somebody had removed his collar.

This had probably been done by Brandreth, who now took charge. Brandreth, whose father had acquired a baronetcy as an ear-specialist, was himself a doctor. He began immediately to assure everyone that Le Bas's condition was not serious.

" The best thing you fellows can do is to clear off home and leave the room as empty as possible," Brandreth said. " I don't want all of you crowding round."

Like most successful medical men in such circumstances, he spoke as if the matter had now automatically passed from the sphere of Le Bas's indisposition to the far more important one of Brandreth's own professional convenience. Clearly there was something to be said for following his recommendation. Brandreth seemed to be handling the

matter competently, and, after a while, all but the more determined began to disappear from the room. Tolland made
a final offer to help before leaving, but Brandreth snapped
at him savagely and he made off; no doubt to appear again
the following year. I wondered how he filled in the time
between Old Boy dinners.

"I shall have to be going, Nick," said Templer. "I have
to get back to the country to-night."

"This dinner seems to have been rather a fiasco."

"Probably my fault," said Templer. "Le Bas never
liked me. However, I think it was really Widmerpool this
time. What's happened to him, by the way? I never had
my chat about Bob."

Widmerpool was no longer in the room. Maiden said
he had gone off to ring up the place where Le Bas was
staying, and warn them what had happened. By then Le
Bas was sitting up and drinking a glass of water.

"Well, fixing old Bob up will have to wait," said
Templer. "I want to do it for Jean's sake. I'm afraid you
had to listen to a lot of stuff about my matrimonial affairs
to-night."

"What are your plans?"

"Haven't got any. I'll ring up some time."

Templer went off. I looked round for Stringham, thinking I would like a word with him before leaving. It was a
long time since we had met, and I was not due to arrive at
Jean's until late. Stringham was not in the small group
that remained. I supposed he had left; probably making
his way to some other entertainment. There was nothing
surprising in that. In any case, it was unlikely that we
should have done more than exchange a few conventional
sentences, even had he remained to talk for a minute or
two. I knew little or nothing of how he lived since his
divorce. His mother's picture still appeared from time to

time in the illustrated papers. No doubt her house in the country provided some sort of permanent background into which he could retire when desirable.

On the way out, I glanced by chance through the door leading to the room where we had dined. Stringham was still sitting in his place at the table, smoking a cigarette and drinking coffee. The dining-room was otherwise deserted. I went through the door and took the chair beside him.

" Hullo, Nick."

" Are you going to sit here all night?"

" Precisely the idea that occurred to me."

" Won't it be rather gloomy?"

" Not as bad as when they were all here. Shall we order another bottle?"

" Let's have a drink at my club."

" Or my flat. I don't want to look at any more people."

" Where is your flat?"

" West Halkin Street."

" All right. I shan't be able to stay long."

" Up to no good?"

" That's it."

" I haven't seen you for ages, Nick."

" Not for ages."

" You know my wife, Peggy, couldn't take it. I expect you heard. Not surprising, perhaps. She has married an awfully nice chap now. Peggy is a really lucky girl now. A really charming chap. Not the most amusing man you ever met, but a really *nice chap*."

" A relation of hers, isn't he?"

" Quite so. A relation of hers, too. He will be already familiar with all those lovely family jokes of the Stepney family, those very amusing jokes. He will not have to have the points explained to him. When he stays at Mountfichet,

he will know where all the lavatories are—if there is, indeed, more than one, a matter upon which I cannot speak with certainty. Anyway, he will not always have to be bothering the butler to direct him to where that one is—and losing his way in that awful no-man's-land between the servants' hall and the gun-room. What a house! Coronets on the table napkins, but no kind hearts between the sheets. He will be able to discuss important historical events with my ex-father-in-law, such as the fact that Red Eyes and Cypria dead-heated for the Cesarewitch in 1893—or was it 1894? I shall forget my own name next. He will be able to talk to my ex-mother-in-law about the time Queen Alexandra made that *double entendre* to her uncle. The only thing he won't be able to do is to talk about Braque and Dufy with my ex-sister-in-law, Anne. Still, that's a small matter. Plenty of people about to talk to girls of Braque and Dufy these days. I heard, by the way, that Anne had got a painter of her own by now, so perhaps even Braque and Dufy are things of the past. Anyway, he's a jolly nice chap and Peggy is a very lucky girl."

"Anne has married Dicky Umfraville."

"Not *the* Dicky Umfraville?"

"Yes."

"Well I never."

Even that did not make much impression on him. The fact that he had not already heard of Anne Stepney's marriage suggested that Stringham must pass weeks at a time in a state in which he took in little or nothing of what was going on round him. That could be the only explanation of ignorance of an event with which he had such close connections.

"Shall we make a move?"

"Where is Peter Templer? I saw his face—sometimes two or three of them—during that awful dinner. We might

bring him along as well. Always feel a bit guilty about Peter."

"He has gone home."

"I bet he hasn't. He's gone after some girl. Always chasing the girls. Let's follow him."

"He lives near Maidenhead."

"Too far. He must be mad. Is he married?"

"His wife has just left him."

"There you are. Women are all the same. My wife left me. Has your wife left you, Nick?"

"I'm not married."

"Lucky man. Who *was* Peter's wife, as they say?"

"A model called Mona."

"Sounds like the beginning of a poem. Well, I should have thought better of her. One of those long-haired painter fellows must have got her into bad habits. Leaving her husband, indeed. She oughtn't to have left Peter. I was always very fond of Peter. It was his friends I couldn't stand."

"Let's go."

"Look here, do let's have another drink. What happened to Le Bas?"

"He is going to be taken home in an ambulance."

"Is he too tight to walk?"

"He had a stroke."

"Is he dead?"

"No—Brandreth is looking after him."

"What an awful fate. Why Brandreth?"

"Brandreth is a doctor."

"Hope I'm never ill when Brandreth is about, or he might look after me. I'm not feeling too good at the moment as a matter of fact. Perhaps we'd better go, or Brandreth will start treating me too. It was Widmerpool's speech, of course. Knocked Le Bas out. Knocked him out

cold. Nearly knocked me out too. Do you remember when we got Le Bas arrested?"

"Let's go to your flat."

"West Halkin Street. Where I used to live before I was married. Surely you've been there."

"No."

"Ought to have asked you, Nick. Ought to have asked you. Been very remiss about things like that."

He was extremely drunk, but his legs seemed fairly steady beneath him. We went upstairs and out into the street.

"Taxi?"

"No," said Stringham. "Let's walk for a bit. I want to cool off. It was bloody hot in there. I don't wonder Le Bas had a stroke."

There was a rich blue sky over Piccadilly. The night was stiflingly hot. Stringham walked with almost exaggerated sobriety. It was remarkable considering the amount he had drunk.

"Why did you have so many drinks to-night?"

"Oh, I don't know," he said. "I do sometimes. Rather often nowadays, as a matter of fact. I felt I couldn't face Le Bas and his Old Boys without an alcoholic basis of some sort. Yet for some inexplicable reason I wanted to go. That was why I had a few before I arrived."

He put out his hand and touched the railings of the Green Park as we passed them.

"You said you were not married, didn't you, Nick?"

"Yes."

"Got a nice girl?"

"Yes."

"Take my advice and don't get married."

"All right."

"What about Widmerpool. Is he married?"

" Not that I know of."

" I'm surprised at that. Widmerpool is the kind of man to attract a woman. A good, sensible man with no nonsense about him. In that overcoat he used to wear he would be irresistible. Quite irresistible. Do you remember that overcoat?"

" It was before my time."

" It's a frightful shame," said Stringham. " A frightful shame, the way these women go on. They are all the same. They leave me. They leave Peter. They will probably leave you. . . . I say, Nick, I am feeling extraordinarily odd. I think I will just sit down here for a minute or two."

I thought he was going to collapse and took his arm. However, he settled down in a sitting position on the edge of the stone coping from which the railings rose.

" Long deep breaths," he said. " Those are the things."

" Come on, let's try and get a cab."

" Can't, old boy. I just feel too, too sleepy to get a cab."

As it happened, there seemed to be no taxis about at that moment. In spite of what must have been the intense discomfort of where he sat, Stringham showed signs of dropping off to sleep, closing his eyes and leaning his head back against the railings. It was difficult to know what to do. In this state he could hardly reach his flat on foot. If a taxi appeared, he might easily refuse to enter it. I remembered how once at school he had sat down on a staircase and refused to move, on the grounds that so many annoying things had happened that afternoon that further struggle against life was useless. This was just such another occasion. Even when sober, he possessed that complete recklessness of behaviour that belongs to certain highly strung persons. I was still looking down at him, trying to decide on the next step, when someone spoke just behind me.

" Why is Stringham sitting there like that?"

It was Widmerpool's thick, accusing voice. He asked the question with a note of authority that suggested his personal responsibility to see that people did not sit about in Piccadilly at night.

"I stayed to make sure everything was done about Le Bas that should be done," he said. "I think Brandreth knows his job. I gave him my address in case of difficulties. It was a disagreeable thing to happen. The heat, I suppose. It ruined the few words I was about to say. A pity. I thought I would have a breath of fresh air after what we had been through, but the night is very warm even here in the open."

He said all this with his usual air of immense importance.

"The present problem is how to get Stringham to his flat."

"What is wrong with him? I wonder if it is the same as Le Bas. Perhaps something in the food——"

Widmerpool was always ready to feel disturbed regarding any question of health. In France he had been a great consumer of patent medicines. He looked nervously at Stringham. I saw that he feared the attack of some mysterious sickness that might soon infect himself.

"Stringham has had about a gallon to drink."

"How foolish of him."

I was about to make some reply to the effect that the speeches had needed something to wash them down with, but checked any such comment since Widmerpool's help was obviously needed to get Stringham home, and I thought it better not to risk offending him. I therefore muttered something that implied agreement.

"Where does he live?"

"West Halkin Street."

Widmerpool acted quickly. He strolled to the kerb. A cab seemed to rise out of the earth at that moment. Per-

haps all action, even summoning a taxi when none is there, is basically a matter of the will. Certainly there had been no sign of a conveyance a second before. Widmerpool made a curious, pumping movement, using the whole of his arm, as if dragging down the taxi by a rope. It drew up in front of us. Widmerpool turned towards Stringham, whose eyes were still closed.

" Take the other arm," he said, peremptorily.

Although he made no resistance, this intervention aroused Stringham. He began to speak very quietly:

" Ah, with the Grape my fading Life provide,
    And wash my Body whence the Life has died . . ."

We shoved him on to the back seat, where he sat between us, still murmuring to himself:

" . . . And lay me shrouded in the living leaf
    By some not unfrequented garden-side . . .

I think that's quite a good description of the Green Park, Nick, don't you. . . . ' Some not unfrequented garden-side ' . . . Wish I sat here more often . . . Jolly nice. . . ."

" Does he habitually get in this state?" Widmerpool asked.

" I don't know. I haven't seen him for years."

" I thought you were a close friend of his. You used to be—at school."

" That's a long time ago."

Widmerpool seemed aggrieved at the news that Stringham and I no longer saw each other regularly. Once decided in his mind on a given picture of what some aspect of life was like, he objected to any modification of the design. He possessed an absolutely rigid view of human

relationships. Into this, imagination scarcely entered, and whatever was lost in grasping the niceties of character was amply offset by a simplification of practical affairs. Occasionally, it was true. I had known Widmerpool involved in situations which were extraordinary chiefly because they were entirely misunderstood, but on the whole he probably gained more than he lost by these limitations; at least in the spheres that attracted him. Stringham now lay between us, as if fast asleep.

" Where is he working at present?"

" I don't know."

" It was a good thing he left Donners-Brebner," said Widmerpool. " He was doing neither himself nor the company any good."

" Bill Truscott has gone, too, hasn't he?"

" Yes," said Widmerpool, looking straight ahead of him. " Truscott had become very interested in the by-products of coal and found it advantageous to make a change."

We got Stringham out of the taxi on arrival without much difficulty and found his latchkey in a waistcoat pocket. Inside the flat, I was immediately reminded of his room at school. There were the eighteenth-century prints of the racehorses, Trimalchio and The Pharisee; the same large, rather florid photograph of his mother: a snapshot of his father still stuck in the corner of its frame. However, the picture of " Boffles " Stringham—as I now thought of him after meeting Dicky Umfraville—showed a decidedly older man than the pipe-smoking, open-shirted figure I remembered from the earlier snapshot. The elder Stringham, looking a bit haggard and wearing a tie, sat on a seat beside a small, energetic, rather brassy lady, presumably his French wife. He had evidently aged considerably. I wondered if friendship with Dicky Umfraville had had anything to do with this. Opposite these photographs was a

drawing by Modigliani, and an engraving of a seventeenth-century mansion done in the style of Wenceslaus Hollar. This was Glimber, the Warringtons' house, left to Stringham's mother during her lifetime by her first husband. On another wall was a set of coloured prints illustrating a steeplechase ridden by monkeys mounted on dogs.

"What are we going to do with him?"

"Put him to bed," said Widmerpool, speaking as if any other action were inconceivable.

Widmerpool and I, therefore, set out to remove Stringham's clothes, get him into some pyjamas, and place him between the sheets. This was a more difficult job than might be supposed. His stiff shirt seemed riveted to him. However, we managed to get it off at last, though not without tearing it. In these final stages, Stringham himself returned to consciousness.

"Look here," he said, suddenly sitting up on the bed, "what is happening? People seem to be treating me roughly. Am I being thrown out of somewhere? If so, where? And what have I done to deserve such treatment? I am perfectly prepared to listen to reason and admit that I was in the wrong, and pay for anything I have broken. That is provided, of course, that I was in the wrong. Nick, why are you letting this man hustle me? I seem for some reason to be in bed in the middle of the afternoon. Really, my habits get worse and worse. I am even now full of good resolutions for getting up at half-past seven every morning. But who is this man? I know his face."

"It's Widmerpool. You remember Widmerpool?"

"Remember Widmerpool . . ." said Stringham. "Remember Widmerpool. . . . Do I remember Widmerpool? . . . How could I ever forget Widmerpool? . . . How could anybody forget Widmerpool? . . ."

"We thought you needed help, Stringham," said Wid-

merpool, in a very matter-of-fact voice. " So we put you to bed."

" You did, did you?"

Stringham lay back in the bed, looking fixedly before him. His manner was certainly odd, but his utterance was no longer confused.

" You needed a bit of looking after," said Widmerpool.

" That time is past," said Stringham.

He began to get out of bed.

" No. . . ."

Widmerpool took a step forward. He made as if to restrain Stringham from leaving the bed, holding both his stubby hands in front of him, as if warming them before a fire.

" Look here," said Stringham, " I must be allowed to get in and out of my own bed. That is a fundamental human right. Other people's beds may be another matter. In them, another party is concerned. But ingress and egress of one's own bed is unassailable."

" Much better stay where you are," said Widmerpool, in a voice intended to be soothing.

" Nick, are you a party to this?"

" Why not call it a day?"

" Take my advice," said Widmerpool. " We know what is best for you."

" Rubbish."

" For your own good."

" I haven't got my own good at heart."

" We will get you anything you want."

" Curse your charity."

Once more Stringham attempted to get out of the bed. He had pushed the clothes back, when Widmerpool threw himself on top of him, holding Stringham bodily there.

While they struggled together, Stringham began to yell at the top of his voice.

" So these are the famous Widmerpool good manners, are they?" he shouted. " This is the celebrated Widmerpool courtesy, of which we have always heard so much. Here is the man who posed as another Lord Chesterfield. Let me go, you whited sepulchre, you serpent, you small-time Judas, coming to another man's house in the guise of paying a social call, and then holding him down in his own bed."

The scene was so grotesque that I began to laugh; not altogether happily, it was true, but at least as some form of nervous relief. The two of them wrestling together were pouring with sweat, especially Widmerpool, who was the stronger. He must have been quite powerful, for Stringham was fighting like a maniac. The bed creaked and rocked as if it would break beneath them. And then, quite suddenly, Stringham began laughing too. He laughed and laughed, until he could struggle no more. The combat ceased. Widmerpool stepped back. Stringham lay gasping on the pillows.

" All right," he said, still shaking with laughter, " I'll stay. To tell the truth, I am beginning to feel the need for a little rest myself."

Widmerpool, whose tie had become twisted in the struggle, straightened his clothes. His dinner-jacket looked more extraordinary than ever. He was panting hard.

" Is there anything you would like?" he asked in a formal voice.

" Yes," said Stringham, whose mood was now completely changed. " A couple of those little pills in the box on the left of the dressing-table. They will knock me out finally. I do dislike waking at four and thinking things

over. Perhaps three of the pills would be wiser, on second thoughts. Half measures are never any good."

He was getting sleepy again, and spoke in a flat, mechanical tone. All his excitement was over. We gave him the sleeping tablets. He took them, turned away from us, and rolled over on his side.

" Good-night, all," he said.

" Good-night, Charles."

" Good-night, Stringham," said Widmerpool, rather severely.

We perfunctorily tidied some of the mess in the immediate neighbourhood of the bed. Stringham's clothes were piled on a chair. Then we made our way down into the street.

" Great pity for a man to drink like that," said Widmerpool.

I did not answer, largely because I was thinking of other matters : chiefly of how strange a thing it was that I myself should have been engaged in a physical conflict designed to restrict Stringham's movements : a conflict in which the moving spirit had been Widmerpool. That suggested a whole social upheaval : a positively cosmic change in life's system. Widmerpool, once so derided by all of us, had become in some mysterious manner a person of authority. Now, in a sense, it was he who derided us; or at least his disapproval had become something far more powerful than the merely defensive weapon it had once seemed.

I remembered that we were not far from the place where formerly Widmerpool had run into Mr. Deacon and Gypsy Jones on the night of the Huntercombes' dance. Then he had been on his way to a flat in Victoria. I asked if he still lived there with his mother.

" Still there," he said. " Though we are always talking

of moving. It has great advantages, you know. You must come and see us. You have been there in the past, haven't you?"

" I dined with you and your mother once."

" Of course. Miss Walpole-Wilson was at dinner, wasn't she? I remember her saying afterwards that you did not seem a very serious young man."

" I saw her brother the other day at the Isbister Retrospective Exhibition."

" I do not greatly care for the company of Sir Gavin," said Widmerpool. " I dislike failure, especially failure in one holding an official position. It is letting all of us down. But—as I was saying—we shall be rather occupied with my new job for a time, so that I expect we shall not be doing much entertaining. When we have settled down, you must come and see us again."

I was not sure if his " we " was the first person plural of royalty and editors, or whether he spoke to include his mother; as if Mrs. Widmerpool were already a partner with him in his bill-broking. We said good-night, and I wished him luck in the Acceptance World. It was time to make for Jean's. She was arriving in London by a late train that evening, again lodged in the flat at the back of Rutland Gate.

On the way there I took from my pocket the postcard she had sent telling me when to arrive. I read it over, as I had already done so many times that day. There was no mistake. I should be there at the time she asked. The events of the evening seemed already fading into unreality at the prospect of seeing her once more.

The card she had sent was of French origin, in colour, showing a man and woman seated literally one on top of the other in an arm-chair upholstered with crimson plush. These two exchanged ardent glances. They were evidently

on the best of terms, because the young man, fair, though at the same time rather semitic of feature, was squeezing the girl's arm just above the elbow. Wearing a suit of rich brown material, a tartan tie and a diamond ring on the third finger of his right hand, his face, as he displayed a row of dazzling teeth, reminded me of Prince Theodoric's profile—as the Prince might have been painted by Isbister. The girl smiled back approvingly as she balanced on his knee.

"Doesn't she look like Mona?" Jean had written on the back. Dark with corkscrew curls, the girl was undeniably pretty, dressed in a pink frock, its short sleeves frilled with white, the whole garment, including the frills, covered with a pattern of small black spots. The limits of the photograph caused her legs to fade suddenly from the picture, an unexpected subordination of design created either to conceal an impression of squatness, or possibly a purely visual effect—the result of foreshortening—rather than because these lower limbs failed in the eyes of the photographer to attain a required standard of elegance. For whichever reason, the remaining free space at the foot of the postcard was sufficient to allow the title of the caption below to be printed in long, flourishing capitals:

> *Sex Appeal*
> *Ton regard et ta voix ont un je ne sais quoi . . .*
> *D'étrange et de troublant qui me met en émoi.*

Although in other respects a certain emptiness of background suggested a passage or hall, dim reflections of looking-glass set above a shelf painted white seemed to belong to a dressing-table: a piece of furniture hinting, consequently, of bedrooms. To the left, sprays of artificial

flowers, red and yellow, drooped from the mouth of a large vase of which the base was invisible. This gigantic vessel assumed at first sight the proportions of a wine vat or sepulchral urn, even one of those legendary jars into which Morgiana, in the Arabian Nights, poured boiling oil severally on the Forty Thieves: a public rather than private ornament, it might be thought, decorating presumably the bedroom, if bedroom it was, of a hotel. Indeed, the style of furnishing was reminiscent of the Ufford.

Contemplating the blended tones of pink and brown framed within the postcard's scalloped edge of gold, one could not help thinking how extraordinarily unlike "the real thing" was this particular representation of a pair of lovers; indeed, how indifferently, at almost every level except the highest, the ecstasies and bitterness of love are at once conveyed in art. So much of the truth remains finally unnegotiable; in spite of the fact that most persons in love go through remarkably similar experiences. Here, in the picture, for example, implications were misleading, if not positively inaccurate. The matter was presented as all too easy, the twin flames of dual egotism reduced almost to nothing, so that there was no pain; and, for that matter, almost no pleasure. A sense of anxiety, without which the condition could scarcely be held to exist, was altogether absent.

Yet, after all, even the crude image of the postcard depicted with at least a degree of truth one side of love's outward appearance. That had to be admitted. Some of love was like the picture. I had enacted such scenes with Jean: Templer with Mona: now Mona was enacting them with Quiggin: Barnby and Umfraville with Anne Stepney: Stringham with her sister Peggy : Peggy now in the arms of her cousin: Uncle Giles, very probably,

with Mrs. Erdleigh : Mrs. Erdleigh with Jimmy Stripling :
Jimmy Stripling, if it came to that, with Jean : and Duport,
too.

The behaviour of the lovers in the plush arm-chair beside
the sparse heads of those sad flowers was perfectly normal;
nor could the wording of the couplet be blamed as specially
far-fetched, or in some other manner indefensible.
" D'étrange et de troublant " were epithets, so far as they
went, perfectly appropriate in their indication of those indefinable, mysterious emotions that love arouses. In themselves there was nothing incongruous in such descriptive
labels. They might, indeed, be regarded as rather apt. I
could hardly deny that I was at that moment experiencing
something of the sort.

The mere act of a woman sitting on a man's knee, rather
than a chair, certainly suggested the Templer *milieu*. A
memorial to Templer himself, in marble or bronze, were
public demand ever to arise for so unlikely a cenotaph,
might suitably take the form of a couple so grouped. For
some reason—perhaps a confused memory of *Le Baiser*—
the style of Rodin came to mind. Templer's own point of
view seemed to approximate to that earlier period of the
plastic arts. Unrestrained emotion was the vogue then,
treatment more in his line than some of the bleakly intellectual statuary of our own generation.

Even allowing a fairly limited concession to its character
as a kind of folk perception—an eternal girl sitting on an
eternal young man's knee—the fact remained that an in-
finity of relevant material had been deliberately omitted
from this vignette of love in action. These two supposedly
good-looking persons were, in effect, going through the
motions of love in such a manner as to convince others, perhaps less well equipped for the struggle than themselves,
that they, too, the spectators, could be easily identified with

some comparable tableau. They, too, could sit embracing on crimson chairs. Although hard to define with precision the exact point at which a breach of honesty had occurred, there could be no doubt that this performance included an element of the confidence-trick.

The night was a shade cooler now. Jean was wearing a white blouse, or sports shirt, open at the neck. Beneath it, her body trembled a little.

" What was your dinner like?" she asked.

" Peter turned up."

" He said he would probably go there."

I told her about Le Bas; and also about Stringham.

" That is why I am a bit late."

" Did Peter mention that Bob is back in England?"

" Yes."

" And that his prospects are not too bad?"

" Yes."

" That may make difficulties."

" I know."

" Don't let's talk of them."

" No."

" Darling Nick."

Outside, a clock struck the hour. Though ominous, things still had their enchantment. After all, as St. John Clarke was reported to have said at the Huntercombes', " All blessings are mixed blessings." Perhaps, in spite of everything, the couple on the postcard could not be dismissed so easily. It was in their world that I seemed now to find myself.

Fontana Books

Fontana is a leading paperback publisher of fiction and non-fiction, with authors ranging from Alistair MacLean, Agatha Christie and Desmond Bagley to Solzhenitsyn and Pasternak, from Gerald Durrell and Joy Adamson to the famous Modern Masters series.

In addition to a wide-ranging collection of internationally popular writers of fiction, Fontana also has an outstanding reputation for history, natural history, military history, psychology, psychiatry, politics, economics, religion and the social sciences.

All Fontana books are available at your bookshop or newsagent; or can be ordered direct. Just fill in the form and list the titles you want.

FONTANA BOOKS, Cash Sales Department, G.P.O. Box 29, Douglas, Isle of Man, British Isles. Please send purchase price, plus 8p per book. Customers outside the U.K. send purchase price, plus 10p per book. Cheque, postal or money order. No currency.

NAME (Block letters)

ADDRESS

While every effort is made to keep prices low, it is sometimes necessary to increase prices on short notice. Fontana Books reserve the right to show new retail prices on covers which may differ from those previously advertised in the text or elsewhere.

Books by Anthony Powell

NOVELS
Afternoon Men
Venusberg
From a View to a Death
Agents and Patients
What's Become of Waring

A DANCE TO THE MUSIC OF TIME
A Question of Upbringing
A Buyer's Market
The Acceptance World
At Lady Molly's
Casanova's Chinese Restaurant
The Kindly Ones
The Valley of Bones
The Soldier's Art
The Military Philosophers
Books Do Furnish a Room
Temporary Kings
Hearing Secret Harmonies

TO KEEP THE BALL ROLLING (MEMOIRS)
Volume I: Infants of the Spring

GENERAL
John Aubrey and His Friends

PLAYS
The Garden God *and* The Rest I'll Whistle

THE ACCEPTANCE WORLD

ANTHONY POWELL was born in London in 1905. His father was a soldier, of a family mostly soldiers or sailors, which moved from Wales about a hundred and fifty years ago. He was educated at Eton and Balliol College, Oxford, of which he is now an Honorary Fellow.

From 1926 he worked for about nine years at Duckworths, the publishers, then as scriptwriter for Warner Brothers in England. During the war he served in the Welch Regiment and Intelligence Corps; acting as Liaison Officer with the Polish, Belgian, Czechoslovak, Free French and Luxembourg forces, being promoted major.

Before and after World War II he wrote reviews and literary columns for various papers, including the *Daily Telegraph* and the *Spectator*. From 1948-52 he worked on the *Times Literary Supplement*, and was Literary Editor of *Punch*, 1952-58.

Between 1931 and 1949, Anthony Powell published five novels, a biography, *John Aubrey and His Friends*, and a selection from Aubrey's works. The first volume of his twelve-volume novel, *A Dance to the Music of Time*, was published in 1951, and the concluding volume, *Hearing Secret Harmonies*, appeared in 1975. In 1976 he published the first volume of his memoirs, *To Keep the Ball Rolling*, under the title *Infants of the Spring*.

In 1934 he married Lady Violet Pakenham, daughter of the fifth Earl of Longford. They have two sons. They live in Somerset, to which they moved in 1952.